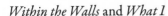 *Within the Walls* and *What I*

MW00608615

UNIVERSITY PRESS OF FLORIDA

Florida A&M University, Tallahassee
Florida Atlantic University, Boca Raton
Florida Gulf Coast University, Ft. Myers
Florida International University, Miami
Florida State University, Tallahassee
New College of Florida, Sarasota
University of Central Florida, Orlando
University of Florida, Gainesville
University of North Florida, Jacksonville
University of South Florida, Tampa
University of West Florida, Pensacola

Within the Walls
and
What Do I Love?

H.D.

Edited by Annette Debo

UNIVERSITY PRESS OF FLORIDA

Gainesville | Tallahassee | Tampa | Boca Raton

Pensacola | Orlando | Miami | Jacksonville | Ft. Myers | Sarasota

Introduction, notes, and bibliography copyright 2014 by Annette Debo
Primary text for *Within the Walls* and *What Do I Love?* by H.D. (Hilda Doolittle),
copyright © 1993 Perdita Schaffner. Copyright © 2014 The Schaffner Family Foundation.
Published by arrangement with New Directions Publishing Corporation, agents.

Printed in the United States of America on acid-free paper

This book may be available in an electronic edition.

21 20 19 18 17 16   6 5 4 3 2 1

First cloth printing, 2014
First paperback printing, 2016

Library of Congress Control Number: 2014937643
ISBN 978-0-8130-6010-1 (cloth)
ISBN 978-0-8130-6204-4(pbk.)

The University Press of Florida is the scholarly publishing agency for the State
University System of Florida, comprising Florida A&M University, Florida Atlantic
University, Florida Gulf Coast University, Florida International University, Florida
State University, New College of Florida, University of Central Florida, University
of Florida, University of North Florida, University of South Florida, and University
of West Florida.

University Press of Florida
15 Northwest 15th Street
Gainesville, FL 32611-2079
http://www.upf.com

To Steve, Zac, and Ben

Contents

Figures

Acknowledgments

The many new editions of H.D.'s writing are fundamentally changing H.D. and modernist studies, and I am pleased to be able to participate in this effort by offering this edition of H.D.'s *Within the Walls* and *What Do I Love?* As always, I have found the H.D. community to be impressively supportive. For their careful reading of this book, I would like to thank Cynthia Hogue and Demetres P. Tryphonopoulos, as well as Susan Stanford Friedman, Marsha Bryant, Susan McCabe, Lara Vetter, Celena E. Kusch, and Rebecca Ann Walsh for many moments of encouragement.

I want to thank my colleagues at Western Carolina University for their support of my scholarly research, particularly consecutive Department Heads Laura Wright and Brian Gastle, as well as Dean Richard D. Starnes. As always, Heidi Buchanan, our remarkable research librarian, has helped me chase many obscure leads and has answered a myriad of peculiar questions with accuracy and precision. A WCU Faculty Research and Creative Activities Grant supported my travel to archives, the building blocks upon which this edition rests.

The bulk of H.D.'s papers—62 boxes at 26.25 linear feet—are held by the Beinecke Rare Book and Manuscript Library at Yale University. The Beinecke's H.D. Fellowship allowed me an uninterrupted month of research there, for which I will be forever grateful. The usefulness of that month was exponentially increased by Nancy Kuhl, Poetry Curator of the Yale Collection of American Literature, whom I thank for her impressive depth of knowledge of the collection, intimate understanding of modernism, and willingness to help me chase seemingly flimsy connections. I have also been able to consult materials held by the Rosenbach Museum and Library, the Bryn Mawr College Library, and the Henry W. and Albert A. Berg Collection of English and American Literature at the New York Public Library.

Thanks are also due to my acquiring editor, Shannon McCarthy, at the University Press of Florida for her unstinting support of this project, her many speedy responses to questions, and her impressive speed in shepherding a manuscript into print! I also appreciate the efforts of Catherine-Nevil Parker and Elizabeth Detwiler, who have smoothed the path and dealt with so many necessary details.

I would like to thank the Schaffner family for their continuing generosity to H.D. scholars, and I particularly thank Valentine Schaffner for allowing me to visit what is known as the Bryher Library at the family home in East Hampton, New York. It was a joy to see the holdings that Perdita Schaffner brought to the United States, and I particularly appreciate Val's willingness to share letters and papers still held and treasured by the family. For permission to quote from H.D.'s, Bryher's, and Perdita Schaffner's unpublished letters, archival materials, and manuscripts (copyright © 2014 by The Schaffner Family Foundation; used by permission of The Schaffner Family Foundation), I am grateful to Declan Spring at New Directions, agent for H.D.'s estate. For permission to quote from published writings, I again thank Declan Spring, New Directions, and The Schaffner Family Foundation (*The Days of Mars* [© Norman Holmes Pearson, 1972]). For permission to quote from Norman Holmes Pearson materials, I thank the Yale Committee on Library Property and Nancy Kuhl, Poetry Curator of the Yale Collection of American Literature. I would also like to thank Britain's Imperial War Museums for permission to use the eight images of World War II posters included in this volume.

This edition began with a birthday present from my father, Thomas Debo, who gave me a rare 1993 edition of *Within the Walls* when I was a graduate student. Although neither of us recognized the import of that present at the time, these then relatively unknown stories shaped my thinking about H.D. and World War II. And as always, my family deserves thanks for their patience and support: to Zac and Ben for balancing my penchant for the calm quiet of research libraries with adrenaline-fueled excitement and to Steve for years of being fun yet responsible.

Editorial Principles

For *Within the Walls*, the H.D. Papers in the American Literature Collection at the Beinecke Rare Book and Manuscript Library, Yale University, hold a typescript copy and a carbon copy, both of which have changes made in H.D.'s hand. Because H.D. made changes on both copies herself, I have incorporated all of her changes. The 1993 edition by Windhover Press selectively applied some of H.D.'s changes from the typescript copy and some of H.D.'s changes from the carbon copy; that edition also excised the final page of the story "Bunny."

For *What Do I Love?* Yale libraries hold H.D.'s rough printed copy, in which H.D. wrote three changes in her own hand. Those corrections were made in the final print run of fifty copies. Thus, the 1950 printing represents her final intentions, and this edition has followed it.

In quotations from letters, which H.D. did not anticipate being published in the same way that she prepared her texts for publication, I have silently corrected obvious spelling and punctuation errors. H.D. was a notoriously awful speller—Marianne Moore once gently suggested that she might consider proofing—but she never meant for her errors to be permanently enshrined in public memory. Because this book is meant for both general readers and scholars, I have chosen the route of readability. In choosing this path, I follow Norman Holmes Pearson, who arranged for publication of many of H.D.'s texts during her lifetime. In those publications, he corrected spelling and punctuation, and he replaced underlining with italics, changes H.D. repeatedly approved. Hard brackets indicate anything that has been added for clarity.

Throughout this edition, minor misspellings in proper nouns have been corrected.

Introduction

R.A.F. day raiders over Berlin's official quarter.

INTO ACTION

"Into Action," ©Imperial War Museums (PST 14882).

London, Capital of the Free World

"London Can Take It!" proclaimed the ten-minute British propaganda film released in 1940, documenting the nightly Nazi bombing of London in an endeavor to entice the Americans out of isolation and into battle in support of the United Kingdom and the rest of Europe.[1] This film captured the iconic images of a London under sharp attack by the Nazi bombers, the British chin-up attitude, and the ruins of a recognizable London. Distributed throughout the Americas and shown widely, this film's defiant attitude portrayed a London that was, in its words, "guarding the frontiers of freedom" and providing a buffer between the United States and the Nazis—a belief that H.D. shared as she endured the critical Battle of Britain in the air from July 10, 1940, to October 31 and the Blitz's direct attacks on London from September 7 to May 10, 1941. Hilda Doolittle—who began signing her work "H.D." early in her career to shield her female identity and her disconcertingly diminutive last name—published her influential imagist book of poetry *Sea Garden* in 1916 and penned an impressive body of work that included poetry, short stories, novels, nonfiction, one children's book, and translations. After growing up in Pennsylvania, H.D. left for Europe in 1911, becoming a member of the expatriate community of modernist writers. She spent World War I in London, and when war again threatened, H.D. once more chose to stay in London, despite the many offers of refuge Americans extended to her and the pressure from her friends and family that she return to relative safety in the United States.

As Bryher—H.D.'s longtime intimate companion—recounts it in her memoir *The Days of Mars*, H.D. said, "It was here that people first read my poetry, . . . I am staying with them."[2] This choice was monumental for H.D.'s writing. Already an established writer but one whose reading public was limited at the beginning of the war, H.D. metamorphosed into a war writer, someone who could capture not only the possibility for healing in her epic *Trilogy* but also the flavor of war-torn London with the authority of a person with her boots on the ground in *Within the Walls* and *What Do I Love?* World War II transformed her into a major writer publishing with Oxford

University Press, Macmillan, Pantheon, Carcanet, and Grove, and she wrote, in part or entirety, some of her most significant works during this war: *Bid Me to Live, The Gift, The Walls Do Not Fall, Tribute to the Angels, The Flowering of the Rod* (the last three books published as *Trilogy*), *Majic Ring, Writing on the Wall* (later combined with *Advent* and published as *Tribute to Freud*), and *By Avon River.* Her artistic production steadily continued after the war as she wrote her late novels, the epic *Helen in Egypt* and additional volumes of poetry, and several memoirs, making the final two decades of her life some of her richest.[3] Bryher described the time: "Now for the 'days of Mars' we were together 'inside the citadel' as many people called London, near the park guns and, though we did not know it then, an unexploded bomb. It is the poets who are the leaders of the people. She could have left us easily, but she stayed."[4]

The most formative months of World War II took place at the beginning, during the Battle of Britain and the Blitz. During these pivotal months between the summer of 1940 and the spring of 1941, H.D. wrote *Within the Walls,* a series of fourteen short stories that capture the atmosphere of London under attack. Presenting the material realities of war, these short stories chronicle H.D.'s experiences during the Blitz. Her firsthand impressions describe a daughter driving a mobile canteen, the tens of thousands of civilian casualties by 1941, the English response to reports of the concentration camps, the nightly Nazi bombing raids, the political climate and Russia's participation, Virginia Woolf's suicide and the role of the artist, and the hope that spring brings. *Within the Walls* also pre-visions and illuminates H.D.'s most famous epic poem *Trilogy,* as well as *The Gift.* H.D. dated each story, excepting two, in this volume with the month and year in which it was written, and she assembled and ordered the stories (the first composed is positioned last in the volume) in the typescript edition she placed in her archive at Yale University that Norman Holmes Pearson, the Yale professor who became her close friend and literary executor, created for her immediately after World War II. Dubbed her "shelf" by Pearson, this archive grew to be the major holding of H.D. papers, including manuscripts, letters, diaries, photographs, personal papers, and more. Because of the assigned dates, these fourteen stories walk readers through the Blitz, bringing them into the world of a London under siege. Previously published only in a limited art edition of 300 copies in 1993 by Windhover Press, *Within the Walls* is here generally available for the first time.

Accompanying these short stories is *What Do I Love?* a series of three long poems about World War II—"May 1943," "R.A.F.," and "Christmas 1944." These poems, written between 1941 and 1944, address the deprivations caused by the shortages, the death of a civilian ambulance driver, a wounded Royal Air Force pilot, and the final Christmas at war.[5] These equally material renderings of the war were described as poems that "reflect life in England during the World War II years and tell of the Battle of Britain" by H.D.'s high school's alumni newsletter.[6] In a 1950 letter to Pearson, H.D. wrote that while these poems did not fit in *Trilogy*, she was fond of them and thought they worked well as a group.[7] *What Do I Love?* was printed in 1950 by the printer of *Life and Letters Today*, as that publication wound to a close. The initial plan was for that printer to set up all of H.D.'s unpublished writings, but that ambitious undertaking was never reached.[8] Instead, *What Do I Love?* became a slim chapbook in a run of fifty copies that H.D. signed and sent to her friends for Christmas that year.

By late 1949 or early 1950, H.D. felt that *What Do I Love?* should be paired with *Within the Walls*. In "H.D. by Delia Alton," H.D. wrote, "We are *Within the Walls*, but only just. This is a series of sketches, written in situ as it were, 1940, 1941. I place 'Before the Battle,' the earliest sketch, dated summer 1940, at the end of *Within the Walls*, as the dream of the mother in the old graveyard at Bethlehem not only pre-visions *The Gift*, the child memoirs, begun about this time, but also acts as an introduction to the selection of poems *What Do I Love* which it now seems to me should be included in this volume."[9] This edition offers these three poems as H.D. grouped them and pairs them with the short stories she thought they complemented.[10]

In order to write this historical and biographical introduction, I plumbed histories, memoirs, and the correspondence among H.D., Bryher, and Perdita Schaffner (H.D.'s daughter, whom Bryher adopted at age nine), as well as their wartime circle in London and friends in the United States. They wrote occasionally to each other and to friends spending the war in Britain or Europe, namely Robert Herring, Norman Holmes Pearson, Sylvia Beach, George Plank, Edith Sitwell, Osbert Sitwell, and Silvia Dobson. However, those friends were enduring the war with them, so often little is mentioned about events or conditions. As Dobson wrote, "In constant danger, we rarely mentioned slaughtered civilians, downed airmen, shattered buildings, the constant threat of invasion and death. . . . One used a great many flippant understatements at that time. In letters we left out scary incidents."[11] These letters, instead, were meant to cheer up their recipients, to silence the bombs bursting around them, and to disregard the hardships. H.D. and Bryher wrote some of their most explanatory letters to American friends and family, to whom they clarified what was going on: why letters were stamped and signed by a censor, why cigarettes could not be shipped to London, how food was being rationed. Bryher once wrote that she so enjoyed meeting an American officer because "he even asked us to tell him about the raids. You daren't mention the subject in an English household because everybody goes one better than yourself about escapes and so on. But he was really impressed with our ruins and our tales."[12] To friends in the United States—Marianne Moore, Viola Baxter Jordan, May Sarton, Kenneth Macpherson, and Mary Herr—and H.D.'s American cousins—Francis Wolle, Clifford Howard, Hattie Howard, and Gretchen Wolle Baker—then, came the most informative letters about the war. All of these materials have enabled me to write an introduction to H.D.'s texts that tells a civilian war story largely in the words of the participants and weaves it into the international events of World War II.

This story takes place in London, after H.D.'s arrival there from Switzerland in 1939, and follows her through the war to the end in May 1945. This introduction addresses Britain's declaration of war and the "Phoney War," Dunkirk and Prime Minister Winston Churchill, the Battle of Britain and the Blitz, realities of life in London, women's war work, concentration camps and refugees, the role of art during wartime, the conscription of women, the Women's Land Army, rationing, a Reading by Famous Poets, D-Day and doodle-bugs, the liberation of Paris, and, finally, V-E Day and the coming of spring.

"Back Them Up!" ©Imperial War Museums (PST 14982).

Living on the Edge of a Volcano

In August 1939, H.D. was in Switzerland at Kenwin—a home she shared with Bryher and their family and whose name was a pun amalgamating "Kenneth" (one of H.D.'s lovers and Bryher's second husband) and "Winifred" (Bryher's given first name)—with Bryher, their housekeeper and friend Elsie Volkart, and their friends from the psychoanalytic community Melitta and Walter Schmideberg.[13] Politically well informed through living near Germany, H.D. and Bryher knew that war was likely. As early as 1933, H.D. wrote in *Writing on the Wall* that she remembered "confetti-like showers" of gold swastikas falling from the sky in Vienna and "death-head chalk-marks" drawn onto the pavement leading to Freud's door;[14] Bryher helped 105 people, Jews and German Christians, escape from Europe and resettle in Britain and the United States;[15] and in 1933 Bryher sent Marianne Moore a piece delineating Nazi atrocities against Jews in Berlin that they both hoped could be placed in the *New York Times*. Silvia Dobson wrote that "both H.D. and Bryher watched with horror as Hitler grew in power while the nearly-senile [Paul von] Hindenberg, President of the Republic, languished. After his death *Mein Kampf* became the national Socialist handbook, while they won elections, their catch-word, Down with Jews. Even then THE FINAL SOLUTION, total extinction of all Jewish people, had been blue-printed. Most Europeans, myself included, remained unaware of the gravity of the situation."[16]

European governments were still following a strategy of German appeasement, and the United States maintained an isolationist policy. The misguided Munich Pact of September 29, 1938, allowed Germany to annex Czechoslovakia, and on September 1, 1939, Germany invaded Poland. In a 1979 letter to Perdita, Melitta Schmideberg described the anxious atmosphere of fall 1939:

> The atmosphere grew increasingly grim and the Swiss were determined to fight. They had issued ration cards as early as 1938. The newspapers were very outspoken about the German danger and they were given an estimate that the Swiss could hold out for three days in their redoubt against the Germans; they were still determined to do so, and

it is believed that it was because of the Swiss determination that the Germans attacked through Belgium. [The Germans] had a marching song . . .

> "and on the way back, we will pocket Switzerland, the little porcupine."

[The Swiss] were surrounded by Fascist countries for most of the war—Germany, Petain's France and Mussolini's Italy, but their determination, coupled with the fact that so many Nazi leaders had put money aside there, probably saved them from invasion, and kept Switzerland as a "neutral" hotbed of spying and intrigue.

. . . We lived somewhat tensely, afraid of Germany invading Switzerland. Hilda and Bryher concentrated on their writing; I took French lessons to pass the time. It was there on September 3rd, that we listened to [Édouard] Daladier's declaration of war for France, and [Neville] Chamberlain's for Britain. . . . Finally at the end of November, we returned to London to the phoney war.[17]

After Britain declared war on Germany on September 3, 1939, H.D. wrote a letter to Clifford Howard that indicates she clearly understood the intricacies of the political scene: "But you can imagine how exciting it is, stimulating of course, as fortunately we get, as with you, much news here, that is censored elsewhere. We even are able to listen-in to Germany—not that we want to. We get London, too, but the English renderings are very solemn and reticent. The French are the most exciting."[18] In November, H.D. returned to London where she would remain for the duration of the war.

The "Phoney War" to which Melitta Schmideberg refers describes the early months of World War II: war had been declared, but no significant offense had been attempted. Germany quickly conquered much of Europe: Finland, Denmark, Norway, Belgium, Holland, and Luxembourg fell. When France was invaded on May 10, 1940, the policy of appeasement was abandoned, Chamberlain resigned, and Winston Churchill was appointed prime minister by King George VI, a choice H.D. approved: "Everyone is very glad old Winston has the job."[19] Robert Herring, editor of *Life and Letters Today*—a literary periodical purchased by Bryher that ran from 1935 to 1950—and a member of H.D.'s chosen family,[20] offered a "salute" in the 1940 "Journal de Guerre" issue of this literary journal in which he lamented the fall of France: "We recognized Paris as the capital of France and of every free man's country as well—the country of the mind. That has no frontiers and knows no distinction of race, recognizing (and with what grace!) only humanity. When you have said 'humanity,' you have stated of what, the world over, France had been felt to be the home."[21]

Under Churchill's leadership, the evacuation of Dunkirk, which lasted from May 28 to June 4, 1940, saved 338,226 soldiers, the core of the British Expeditionary Force (BEF) and many French soldiers. Although Dunkirk in reality represented a brutal defeat in terms of loss of life, ships, aircraft, and heavy equipment, Churchill deemed it a miracle, and the press focused on the triumphant nature of the evacuation and the preservation of nearly 340,000 troops, who then returned to defend Britain. In the same 1940 issue of *Life and Letters Today*, Herring concurred: "Dunkirk was a miracle. Like so many, it involved martyrdom. Up in London again, at the bottom of my row, I see the 'little boats,' returned from that Resurrection regatta. They rock at anchor. How many of my friends did they carry?"[22] H.D. also wrote of the "little ships." In addition to the huge military transport boats and the air cover provided by the Royal Air Force (RAF), civilians had been encouraged to sail in whatever ships they could to help evacuate the troops: "We learn of the little boats and big boats, like a 'regatta' across the channel that has brought the men home from the Dunkirk beaches. . . . Children, boys of 15 went over in old fishing boats with their fathers and helped. Every kind of boat sent out, yachts, old tramps, little private motor-boats." The numbers she shared are close to currently accepted figures: "There were almost 1000 boats, fire-boats, fishing-boats, yachts, merchant marine, little pleasure boats doing the ferry-act the last days. . . . Roughly 335,000 got back . . . and about 30,000 lost, missing and wounded." She also related amazing stories of soldiers arriving safely in Britain under their own power: "The little channel or rather coast pleasure boats, Brighton Queen, Daisy Bell and that sort of thing, went on back and forth through all the mines and bombardments. Some French soldiers have drifted in on a raft, one Englishman, captured, got away, slept in a bush, borrowed some refugee clothes, walked to the coast, rowed across, alone in a little row-boat he found, on the beach."[23]

Although Dunkirk was a military disaster, the presentation of it through heroic stories, especially those involving civilians, lifted hopes high: "We are in terrific form or fettle or mettle or whatever the word is," wrote H.D., and she, along with all of Britain, braced to fight: "I don't want to be O U T of it, at all, and I feel though there is a great drive on, as to air-attack because of getting children out of coast towns, that the thing itself becomes less of a terror and menace each day, as the R.A.F. and the French bring them down literally in hundreds a week. . . . One pilot ran out of ammunition and was so mad that he simply did stunts on the tail of a Heinke or Messer and worried the crew so much that it crashed. . . . It must be this holy war."[24] As opposed to World War I, much of World War II took place on British soil, enlisting the help of civilians, and the line separating civilians and soldiers often blurred. H.D., like many people living in Britain, felt that they were active participants in this war, fighting a just war against an invading, oppressive enemy.

Churchill fostered this participatory attitude in his famed "We Shall Fight on the Beaches" speech:

> Even though large tracts of Europe and many old and famous States have fallen or may fall into the grip of the Gestapo and all the odious apparatus of Nazi rule, we shall not flag or fail. We shall go on to the end, we shall fight in France, we shall fight on the seas and oceans, we shall fight with growing confidence and growing strength in the air, we shall defend our Island, whatever the cost may be, we shall fight on the beaches, we shall fight on the landing grounds, we shall fight in the fields and in the streets, we shall fight in the hills; we shall never surrender, and even if, which I do not for a moment believe, this Island or a large part of it were subjugated and starving, then our Empire beyond the seas, armed and guarded by the British Fleet, would carry on the struggle, until, in God's good time, the New World, with all its power and might, steps forth to the rescue and the liberation of the old.[25]

H.D. reported to Bryher, who was still in Switzerland, that "Old Winston made a stirring speech, reported on radio last night. We are to fight 'on the beaches, on the landing grounds and in the streets' before giving in, though he remarks he does not think this will be literally necessary, as he counted the unparalleled tragedy around Dunkirk, mitigated by 'air victory' which made the feats of the crusaders seem not only far distant but common-place and banal. . . . I live everyday as if it were the last . . . the tempo or pulse of life is speeded up, certainly." She repeated this sentiment often, writing in another letter: "I think it is very stimulating and I live each day, saying 'well I am alive, now what shall I make of these hours.'" In a June 7 letter to Bryher, H.D. referred to David Low's cartoon published on June 6, 1940, in the *Evening Standard*. It featured Adolf Hitler preparing to ring a victory bell, Joseph Goebbels glancing up from a newspaper, and the caption "We have gone too far, Adolf. Der British have declared war." The national hyperbole gripping

Britain is evident in her own words: "The battle of the ports was something out of all time, wonderful. The merchant marine came in for a lot of glory. Tugs were all taken off the Thames, all fire-boats, trawlers, fishing smacks, life-boats and so on, took that terrible trip over and over. Not one British or French soldier was left behind on the beaches."[26] Unfortunately, soldiers were left behind, and Hitler was still intent on conquering all of Europe.

An armistice between France and Germany was signed on June 22, 1940, and Hitler's attention turned to Britain. After unsuccessfully trying to negotiate peace on his own terms, Hitler formulated a plan to invade Britain—Operation Sea Lion—that depended on first neutralizing the RAF. In July, Hitler's speech to the Reichstag "A Last Appeal to Reason" was dropped in propaganda leaflets in Britain. The Ministry of Information countered with its own pamphlets like "If the Invader Comes: What to Do—and How to Do It," which Bryher saved: "The Germans threaten to invade Great Britain. If they do so they will be driven out by our Navy, our Army and our Air Force. Yet the ordinary men and women of the civilian population will also have their part to play. Hitler's invasions of Poland, Holland and Belgium were greatly helped by the fact that the civilian population was taken by surprise. They did not know what to do when the moment came. *You must not be taken by surprise.* This leaflet tells you what general line you should take."[27] As the civilians braced for war—"so pitiless, so irreparable"—the Battle of Britain began in July 1940.[28]

"Never Was So Much Owed by So Many to So Few," ©Imperial War Museums (PST 14972).

This Burning Light of Life

H.D. wrote "Before the Battle," the story positioned last in *Within the Walls*, during the tumultuous summer of 1940.[29] In July, Hitler made plans to invade Britain with a target date of September 15. In order to cripple the RAF, the Battle of Britain began with raids by the Luftwaffe—then regarded as the superior air power—on shipping in the English Channel in July and a blockade of the British Isles in August. The German raids began during the daytime, and the British will to fight was strong: "The B.B.C., I think very fine, with startling first-hand accounts of air-observers and so on. Old Winston was in great form the other night. He keeps telling us how we will 'fight in the streets' and I think many people are looking forward to it," H.D. wrote to Bryher in July.[30] Marianne Moore—the American poet and editor whom H.D. met while at Bryn Mawr College and with whom she reconnected while editing the *Egoist* in 1915—assured H.D. that in the United States "the feeling for England here, is intense,"[31] and H.D. sent positive reports to Bryher in Switzerland: "Very happy—over 60 enemy planes shot down yesterday. Waves seem to come over but no further—knock on wood—than the coast. Comparatively few losses this end. . . . Broke off to listen to the evening news, apparently about 400 planes were over coast & channel to-day, some more shot down, but the last two days they give the astonishing figure as 127 enemy planes destroyed. They are browsing along ports and out for ships—don't know if they don't WANT to get near or can't. Anyhow morale here is very fine."[32]

In the whole of the Battle of Britain, the RAF fought so brilliantly that they changed the course of the war, for which they were justly acclaimed; they provided the first real defeat for the Nazis. On August 20, 1940, Prime Minister Winston Churchill gave a speech offering the famous line "never was so much owed by so many to so few" to describe the debt owed by his country to the RAF. In May H.D. had written Bryher expressing the widely held belief that Hitler would resist bombing London: "I do not think they will come over, as Hit[ler] fears his lovely new art-buildings may be bombed in retaliation. That apparently is what keeps him or may keep him off London—funny but authentic."[33] Unfortunately, on August 24, the Germans, some historians believe accidentally, bombed a church in the Cripplegate area of London, and Churchill immediately ordered the bombing of Berlin on August 26. In retaliation, the Germans began bombing London on August 30—marking a week that changed the direction of the war. Herring thought little of this tit-for-tat approach: "To-morrow I shall read in the papers that our planes were over Germany, whilst enemy raiders attacked our coasts. Would it be only in a dark room, with the balloon barrage shining in the heat-wave beyond the drawn curtains, that I would be tempted to think it seems simpler if both sides stayed home and bombed themselves?"[34] Although the dates of the Battle of Britain and the London Blitz overlap, the shift was one of tactic, from attempting to subdue Britain in preparation for invasion—the date for which was indefinitely postponed—to punishing attacks on civilian as well as military targets in London and other British cities. During the Blitz, which officially began on September 7, London was bombed consecutively for fifty-seven nights; one million London homes were damaged or destroyed; forty thousand civilians were killed, half in London. Much of the city was damaged, including the British Museum, the Houses of Parliament, St. James' Place, St. Paul's Cathedral, and Holland House of the London Library.

As with Dunkirk, these attacks on the civilian population created a very different atmosphere in this war than in World War I. The entire citizenry felt itself critical to the war effort because Hitler was attacking them directly; there was little experiential gulf between the fighting forces and citizens. Bryher commented to a soldier that the night bombings made the populace irascible, and he replied, "'that applies to civilians' then we both thought and he said 'but who are civilians?' And that is so true here, everybody has been shot over at least once and mostly far more often. And life is worse often for us than for the people labeled as forces. It is a funny, upside down world."[35] Similarly, Bryher wrote to Pearson:

> Yes, this is a total war, and one where the civilians have often had more experiences than the so-called soldiers. I know of children of eight who helped put out incendiary bombs in the middle of an air raid with bombs bursting about them. The one unforgettable experience here were the Londoners in the 1940 blitz. They walked through bombs with their shopping baskets and clustered up by the guns in the park as if it were a ball game, to applaud. There is quite a little feeling here,

you know, we civilians feel that we have been bombed and machine gunned, and have had to get to work through black out and with little food. There used to be a joke around, "join the army and have a rest."[36]

H.D. confirmed that even if the First World War was the formative war for her literary generation, the second war created equally powerful sensibilities: "I am very sorry that my letters have been so dull, but things here, you must gather from radio and old papers, have been very intense. I never came near feeling the old war, as I felt this, quite personally."[37] She expressed this sentiment more powerfully to Howard: "We are truly an army, so unlike the last war, where we stood helpless while all the youth of the world was sacrificed for us."[38] H.D. carried this attitude into her life. Perdita confirmed her resolution, in a passage quoted in its entirety below, that "nobody, we might have thought, could be more unsuited to bombardment than my mother. After September 7th, she never mentioned her nerves." H.D.'s letters document that she consistently assured friends and family that she was safe when she was not, that she had enough food when she was hungry, and that she was cheerfully looking forward to victory, which was long in question. She adopted the British chin-up attitude and entered this war clear-eyed and well informed. She did what she could for friends even less well off, like Sylvia Beach, and the war provided grist for her writing, but at a cost she understood.

While Perdita did not complete the book-length memoir about her mother that her son Valentine Schaffner has said she planned and the family was taught to expect, she did leave some lovely passages, in addition to her many published articles. In her unfinished memoir, Perdita wrote an insightful account of 1940 worth quoting here at length because it is otherwise unavailable:

"We may not say, calmly and confidently, that Hitler has missed the bus." Neville Chamberlain, in the spring of 1940.

The bus ripped into Norway, Denmark, Holland, Belgium, and France.

I poured tea in railway stations, and read two classic best sellers, *War and Peace* and *Gone with the Wind* similar in theme: the outbreak of war, high hopes, bravado, and glamour—young men in their uniforms, girls in ball gowns. Followed by escalation, encroachment; an inexorable force, strewing wreckage, taking over everybody's life.

Now it was happening to us. The Battle of Britain. Spitfires, Hurricanes, Messerschmidts tearing around over Southern England, fall out in people's back yards. Few of the enemy planes ever got to London.

Occasionally we would look up and glimpse tiny silver insects wheeling, darting, a puff of smoke, the white dot of a parachute.

The first raids were little more than forays. A lone plane—we came to recognize the guttural vroom-vroom of the engine—circling, going away. A distant bump now and then, way off on the outskirts. We became accustomed to the sirens. Dogs and cats hated them, heard them before we did, cowered and bolted.

September 7. It all came down. The warnings were immediately followed by screeches and the loudest explosions I had ever heard. My apartment building rocked. The bangs came nearer, even louder. I hauled pillows into my windowless kitchenette, closed the door, settled in.

No more close calls. Din and mayhem continued through the night, however—fearful crashes all over town, the clanging of fire engines and ambulances, bursts of anti-aircraft fire. I dozed off, and woke to the high monotone of the All Clear.

"This is the BBC Home Service, London—Richard Dimbleby speaking from the top of St. Paul's." In years to come he would cover Elizabeth's coronation. He described dockland fires still raging, wide spread devastation with dead and wounded as yet uncounted. He spoke emotionally and at length: This is LONDON.

Yes, this was it, really and truly happening to *us*.

There were two sunsets that evening, one in the East from the unquenched glow of burning docks, an ideal target for bombers. They returned that night and every night, through the week, for many weeks.

LONDON CAN TAKE IT! An irksome slogan, what else could London do?

More to the point: lunch and dinner served as usual unless a bomb falls on the building.

A store with all its windows swept into the gutter: Open rather more than usual.

As usual in the midst of the catastrophically unusual. Soon, it seemed to be all we knew. Each day might be our last, whether in Whitechapel or Buckingham Palace. Nothing for it but to take the nights as they came, then pick up and get on with the business of the day. People watched out for each other, British reserve broke down, strangers opened up and communicated. Workers went to work, housewives attended to their duties.

My mother had been in London all along. Bryher stayed on in Switzerland. Then, restless in that peaceful neutral country surrounded by enemy forces, she applied for repatriation. And set off on a circuitous journey in sealed buses, through unoccupied France and Spain, wait listed for a plane out of Lisbon. Incommunicado from start to finish. "Don't worry," Osbert Sitwell said to us, "she'll arrive with the invasion barges."

Winston Churchill gave one of his rousing speeches—with an aside often quoted in later years, not heard by listeners at the time, "and we'll fight them with beer bottles because that's all we've got."

Bryher was at the door a couple of days later.

She moved into my mother's apartment in Lowndes Square, the two of them close together as they had never been before. The place wasn't big enough.

Bryher's energy was prodigious, now it had nowhere to go. She should have been running a platoon, if only she could find one to suit her talents. She wrote letters compulsively, ten to twenty a day. She was on the telephone, constantly, or it was ringing again. Everything echoed.

Nobody, we might have thought, could be more unsuited to bombardment than my mother.

After September 7th, she never mentioned her nerves.

Her mornings were orderly and serene, consecrated to work. She wrote a long poem, *The Walls Do Not Fall*, which eventually became a trilogy.

Bryher channeled her executive powers into keeping house. She reviewed the events of the night with Hodge the doorman, and as soon as the shops opened, she set off with a clutch of string bags and made the rounds. Also made friends chatting up the staff, hearing their bomb stories.

She was genuinely interested in people, how they lived, how it all was for them; she remembered every detail—Mum's arthritis, sister Betty the landgirl digging potatoes in Essex, Dad's duties as an air raid warden—the broken windows, the scares, the troubles. They in turn responded to the austere little figure always there at the same time every day. They stashed extras aside—previous chocolate biscuits, a jar of Bovril. Then over to the fish monger—yes, some nice Finnan Haddie, just in, handy for supper. On to the baker, sometimes he had scones, sometimes not, anyway his bread was better than most. And so it went, methodically, diligently. It took quite a lot of time. Home, laden like a pack pony. She unloaded in the kitchen and went out again to meet Osbert Sitwell for their daily walk in the park. . . .

Was I ever scared? YES! At times, by no means all the time. In the line of fire, always. Whenever I heard that long whistle as of giant shears ripping down a mile high bolt of silk—followed by violent explosion. And another and another, six in a row, each getting nearer. A scary count down as even the most hardened battle veterans admitted. Delayed action bombs came singly, the same silky descent with a dud landing—home evacuated on the instant, streets cordoned off while new age heroes tinkered with fuses. Land mines, chained to parachutes. Clank, clank, hither and thither with the wind, megablast over a horrendous radius.

Then, one night in late November, rain on the window pane, searchlights criss-crossing the sky, the nine o'clock news as depressing as ever. But no sirens. We waited endlessly, couldn't settle down. The silence was totally disorienting. It took us at least a week to adjust.

The lull continued until the eve of New Year's Eve, when the entire sky turned crimson under a brief but massive attack of fire bombs. St. Paul's was saved that night, only just.[39]

Bryher agreed with Perdita's description of life in London: "'London can take it' was not a slogan, it was a statement of fact. The bombing that October seemed continuous. Some people pretended that it was not happening at all, others endured hours of uncomfortable travel daily in order to spend the night in the supposedly safer countryside. The majority of us, however, 'got on with it.'"[40]

H.D. remained in London except for occasional excursions to the countryside and got on with it. She resided in her flat at 10 Lowndes Square, as described in better times by Dobson:

These modern blocks of six story well-designed luxury flats stand on the west side of a tree-lined square, actually an oblong area, where Regency and Victorian houses used to face one another across spacious central gardens, surrounded by iron railings, with locked gates of which the residents had keys. From the south end of Lowndes Square a road leads to Belgravia, and to a mews, Kinnerton Place, where Kenneth Macpherson lived. From the north end, two roads branch off, giving entry to busy Knightsbridge with Albert Gate, entrance to Hyde Park, on its further side. Hundreds of London enclaves vied with one another, sporting plane and pine trees, blossoming May, Lilac, Cherry, Laburnum, syringa, rising from dense laurel, privet, hydrangea bushes. Sometimes there were gardener's sheds; always winding gravel paths edged with lawns, spring bulbs, summer annuals, clumps of heather, ground cover, trailing ivy. From her fourth-floor dining-room window, H.D. looked out on these gardens. Her sitting-room, kitchen and bed-room faced south-west, with views over the two-story Sloane Street shops towards Harrods tall façade, flanked by office buildings, a church or two, distinctive Victorian mansions.[41]

H.D.'s flat also offered a spare bedroom, into which Bryher moved for the du-ration of the war when she arrived in London on September 28, 1940.

Bryher, in danger for her work with refugees, had fled Switzerland with one suitcase, food for the journey, and the small amount of cash allowed to leave the country. With forty-four other people, she set out on a fraught journey to Lisbon, where she was stranded for weeks, almost penniless, before being allowed to fly to Britain.[42] For both H.D. and Bryher and the visitors they often housed, the building at Lowndes Square provided protec-tion. H.D. wrote to Moore that "we have been so very lucky and have such a marvelous sort of fortress in this block of apartments; a new block with steel girders and we sleep, as I think I told you in a nice box room on the ground floor."[43] Moore thanked her for the reassurance—"How grateful we are for the reassurance about the building you are in and its reliable walls. I have longed to ask but really couldn't bring myself to"—and offered wishes for ice, fog, and rain, weather that confounded the German bombers.[44] Al-though she passed by bombed apartment buildings daily, H.D.'s remained fortuitously intact, for which she was constantly thankful: "Life is so beauti-ful—and chairs and tables so important and every day one is so grateful for the wall about one, the roof, the unbroken windows."[45] Early on in the Blitz, H.D. and Bryher would retire to their storage space in the basement, the box room H.D. describes to Moore, which they furnished with beds, a portable radio, and a tea kettle, but as the war dragged on and the continuous priva-tions became increasingly tiresome, H.D. risked sleeping in her own com-fortable bed, and visitors were given the box room.

In September, H.D. shared her resolve with Howard: "It is very sad but the world can't continue with that band of ill-bred deluded barbarians about, and the sooner they quietly and quickly disappear the better for us all—I had not this feeling in the last war, but now it is a clear case of survival, at stake." The tribulations that would last at least until the war's end, and some well beyond, had already begun, as H.D. describes the sirens, blackouts, and the new odyssey of finding food: "Now there is a siren going again, the day-time ones never worry me and at night, I am snug in the little dug-out on the ground floor, but it is always an interruption to shopping and so on. One has to dash out, when one can, and between that and constant black-out precautions, pasting up fresh black-paper and so on, one has one's days' and nights' work cut out for one. Each day, however, seems a special gift, to be filled full . . . it is a pity that it takes such heart-breaking condition[s] to bring one to the fullest realization of the sanctity of each minute."[46]

This sense of thankfulness was created by the constant danger; H.D. confided to Moore that "death becomes the one important idea—and that idea is so familiar."[47] Empathy poured from Moore, who stayed in close touch with H.D. and Bryher throughout the war: "Our hearts are torn by the word each day of unpity for those persons and those things we love in London, and today word of the children lost in mid ocean. The fire of resolution kindled by these things, the valor and self control of everyone in England, make the wickedness seem the more intense." Moore often thanked them for sharing personal testimony about life in London: "You and Hilda in your letters are so vivid,—'the sublime heroism of the masses,' the extraordinary subway stairs you mention, lined with sleeping children, the unnatural danger of the blackout; and the obstacles to getting a job. When one is panting with desire to help the country win, and what is more rare—equipped at every point as you are, to do it—I know the white hot intensity of some of your wartime reflections. But there is a certain consolation, don't you think, in the sense that each of us is scourged with the very same sense of frustration,—an illusion after all, Bryher. What we *feel* are the sinews of war."[48] By December 1940, Moore had begun sending packages of food, since malnutrition and starvation were a new reality in Britain and even more so on the continent. She asked H.D. what she would like: "Raisins? Chocolates? Cigarettes and if so what kind? Some cans of vegetable juice—V-8 for instance which combines several juices in one."[49] The packages would keep coming throughout the war, but with more prosaic contents.

The realities of war were carefully inscribed into Negley Farson's illustrated *Bomber's Moon*, which sought to share the reality of life in London during the Blitz—a book H.D. read and recommended to friends. Farson's goal was to record the character of London, before this city was irrevocably altered by the bombing. Farson describes the shelters in subway stations and church crypts, the limited food supplies, the bomb stories, and the charitable nature of Londoners. His portraits are of ordinary people, their words recorded in local dialects. This literary and visual portrait of London was meant to offer courage: "The scene of these unworried people calmly getting ready to face an invader who had threatened to exterminate them . . . was enough to convince any observer that when England wants strong material in sheer manhood, she still has the tough stuff. That is the feeling I brought back from the gentleness, the humour, the unbeatable spirit I saw along Britain's walls. You are an invincible nation—and, in your hearts, you know it."[50]

Other inspirational stories were offered by government publications, which H.D. also avidly read, recommended, and sent to Americans when materials were allowed abroad. This information, which naturally crossed the line into propaganda, was disseminated by the Ministry of Information, a governmental department officially formed the day after Britain declared war but quietly begun in the mid-1930s given the expectation of another war. In World War I, this job had been shared by several departments, whose joint efforts had produced confusion and misinformation. This new single department was meant to ameliorate those problems and had three primary tasks: censoring the press, disseminating information in Britain, and providing information to the Allies and neutral countries like Switzerland. In particular, H.D. recommended the 1940 "The Battle of Britain" and praised the 1942 *Front Line* as "a beautifully written clear statement of the whole 'Battle'" to friends like Dobson, Jordan, and Francis Wolle.[51] These detailed accounts tell the war story from a British vantage point.

As Perdita confirmed, the attacks increased at the year's end. The Second Great Fire of London occurred in December 1940 as the result of German air raids; 10,000 bombs fell on London on December 29, and Paternoster Row, the heart of London's publishing industry, burned. Dobson laments the loss, which eerily mimicked the Nazis' purposeful book purges: "A tragedy none of us will ever forget was the destruction of half London's publishing houses in one savage raid. They were probably trying for The Admiralty or No 10 Downing Street. Such a burning of books distressed us all."[52] In an early 1941 "News Reel," Herring wrote,

So many publishers have taken part in the move to the West End, that I think many of us had forgotten how many still remained near St.

Paul's. If we had, the City fire will have reminded us. Many firms were burnt out. Simpkin, Marshall, the great wholesalers, alone lost three and a half million copies. Longmans, Green and Co. had taken the precaution of dispersing their stocks; unfortunately, both their storage places, though in different parts of London, were destroyed the same night. . . . Very quickly, more fortunate publishers came to such victims' aid, but vast stocks have been lost. . . . Therefore, till many volumes come again into print, we must keep books in the forefront of our mind. Not only to help the hard-hit trade in which we are most interested; not only to keep clear a channel of expression of thought; but to preserve in ourselves the habit of being familiar with the fruits of thought, of equipping ourselves with knowledge and the power to absorb knowledge. For it is from those who have no standards of comparison, no width in their outlook, and no depth to their outpourings that will come most of the troubles of the near future, no less than have come those of the immediate past.[53]

H.D. and Bryher partook in the effort to collect replacement books for the bombed libraries, but their efforts were hampered by the competing Books for Battle campaign, the need for paper in munitions production that led to "the pulping down of very uninteresting books—though I am afraid in the process, much of interest has gone to scrap. We love our old books now so much more, as we are able to appreciate the good paper and print."[54]

Still, the populace, whom H.D. likened to limpets sticking to rocks, "a tough set," fought for its city.[55] H.D. shared a story with George Plank, an American friend living in England who illustrated her 1936 book *The Hedgehog*: "It is good the way every one now—but everyone—is a fireman. Did you hear of the child in a party-dress who rushed into a neighbor's house & *jumped* on the incendiary in her little party slippers? Put it out, too, and no harm done the slippers!"[56] She assured her cousin Gretchen Wolle Baker that "Harrods is o.k., they had bombs in Basil Street right in front of the side door, but not a window even smashed, and once a bomb through the top, but no one noticed it, as they simply shut up the top floor while they cleared up."[57] To a friend from her Philadelphia youth who, like H.D., knew Ezra Pound and William Carlos Williams, Viola Baxter Jordan, H.D. wrote, "We do live in a strange way—it's a sort of continued night-mare; all London is technically 'danger-zone,' though we have been all right, luckily. . . . Sorry this is so dull, but there is little to write of, I mean our daily ESCAPE is our great adventure—and as I say, that must seem strange and you take it for granted, naturally."[58]

At the end of 1940, the short propaganda film *Christmas Under Fire*—which Herring covered in *Life and Letters Today*—was released by the British government. In the same vein as *London Can Take It* (even sharing the same narrator, Quentin Reynolds), *Christmas Under Fire* showcased the resilience of the British populace as well as their suffering, juxtaposing holly with barbed wire, tinsel with guns. The film focuses on a family pulled apart by the war, and it portrays their attempts at revelries while the troops watch for enemy planes: "Christmas here this year won't perhaps be the Christmas children in America will be lucky enough to enjoy. England is fighting for her life, and even the smallest child understands that." No bells can ring on Christmas because the bells are only to be rung on the occasion of an invasion; people pray for storms, even when they obscure the Christmas star, because inclement weather slows the German bombers. The film ends with Christmas hymns and shots of people sheltering in subway tunnels, decorated with meager Christmas trees and cheer. Reynolds intones, "today England stands unbeaten, unconquered, unafraid," and the call to action is unmistakable.

As an American supporting the British, H.D. was embarrassed that her country was not rushing to enter the war, and she tried to clarify British attitudes for her American friends: "By the way there is *NO* such talk as you mention about people here saying they are fighting the war for USA—that is sheer fifth column or pro-Nazi propaganda. They do all they can, in very subtle ways, to break across any entente—the same things went on in France, posters etc. pasted up, blaming Great Britain for the fate of France—absolute rot—please realize that that is all rot, I see masses of people of all kinds and they are so GRATEFUL to USA for the 'tools' and help with children over there and with food."[59] What Britain really needed was for the United States to enter the war.

"Women Wanted as Ambulance Drivers," ©Imperial War Museums (PST 3399).

Intra Muros: Within the Walls

During the first months of 1941, H.D. was living through the Blitz while writing the short stories in *Within the Walls*. This volume is autobiographical and remained unpublished during H.D.'s life. Some of its characters are identifiable even under their fictional references: the narrator is H.D.; "the girl" is Perdita; Bee is Bryher; Elfrida is the aristocratic, flamboyant poet Edith Sitwell; Jo is H.D.'s friend Silvia Dobson, named after the tomboy and would-be writer Jo in Louisa May Alcott's *Little Women*; "he" in "The Ghost" is Osbert Sitwell, Edith's brother. However, some of the characters retain their actual names—George is George Plank; Robert is Robert Herring; Dr. Walter is Walter Schmideberg—something H.D. would most likely have rectified had she published this text during her lifetime because she herself strongly objected to being identified by name in writings by others. Some of these stories are materialist renderings of civilian life during wartime, some are more philosophical dream sequences, and these external and internal stories combine to form a comprehensive portrait of civilian life during the war. In "H.D. by Delia Alton," H.D. emphasizes that in this volume "the sketches 'come alive,' they are actually happening, and the dreams 'dream true.'"[60] This introduction considers two of H.D.'s overarching concerns—time and the role of the writer—but its focus remains on the conditions of war. H.D. infuses her stories with specific material references that resonate autobiographically and historically, resonances traced here. Additionally, four stories emphasize themes particularly pertinent in the context of World War II: "Bunny" claims that the world is radically changing for women, "Escape" considers Nazi atrocities, "The Ghost" addresses the future of art, and "Before the Battle" offers hope through the Persephone/Demeter myth.

The story "Within the Walls" opens H.D.'s volume by ruminating on time: "the whole conception of time must be re-valued" (107). In war, time worked differently, on both psychic and practical levels. For H.D., time felt different in how it passed, how she valued it, and even in its musical tone. She wrote Jordan that "after last autumn's Blitzes, we all feel as if time were so relative, one understands Eddington and Einstein at long last."[61] Sir Arthur Stanley Eddington, a British astrophysicist, interpreted Albert Einstein's Theory of Relativity for a lay audience, explaining the relationship between space and time, which was no longer viewed as a simple linear measurement of experience. These new scientific theories about how time functions offered insights to H.D. because time, for people within the walls in London, moved differently than for those outside of the walls. The constant awareness of death changed H.D.'s sense of time: "hour is cut from hour in precious prismatic fragments" (108). Each hour was prized because she was still not only within the walls of London but also the walls of her own body; she was still alive.

Time is also a theme in the story "Pattern," in which the narrator has left behind a traveling clock that she wants back, a clock that measures time while she is moving from place to place. Her mother appears in this story, and she refuses to let the narrator return to find her clock. For H.D., a consummate traveler, a travel clock would be a necessity, and its difference would be in its construction—small, light, and battery-operated. But it is in motion that time measures differently—how people move through space determines the speed of time, according to Einstein. The mother emphasizes a design in a tapestry that belongs to the narrator, and, significantly, while the needlework may not be superior, "the pattern is not broken" (111). The pattern is one of waves—not unlike time waves—and it continues throughout the piece, becoming more definitive toward the end, as if the future has already been written on some level of existence. Throughout her body of work, H.D. describes life and experience as cyclical like a nautilus shell, which turns in consistent but slightly larger curves with each rotation. H.D.'s waves inscribe a similar rhythm into life, and at the story's end, the narrator finds her clock, which has returned to her and is "ticking away," measuring away the seconds of life (111). Time also dominates "Dream of a Book" with the question: "This race with time—who is going to win? There are already 40,000 civilian casualties" (113). Which nation can buy enough time to win? Which nation can kill the other in less time? Time is now being measured in numbers of the dead, rather than in seconds or speed of motion. In "Tide-Line," H.D. connects the fourth dimension, for Einstein of time and for her of vision and dream, to blue light, which she here defines as "high-powered thought" (121). It is her connection to this dimension that allows her to write, to exist in the real world of war and the vision world, crucial to writing, simultaneously.

A second concern in *Within the Walls* is the role of the writer. For H.D., reading and writing are as important as food. Writing, in "Dream of a Book," is juxtaposed with listening: the narrator "can not listen" nor can she "not not-listen" to the constant bombing (113). Her option is to plug her ears, which removes her into a different dimension of existence, one she likens to "snow falling. It was as quiet as that" (113). She explains that after one blitz night, one ear bled, the sound was so intense. H.D. had packed a bag of essentials in case she had to evacuate quickly, a bag that included "the wax ear-plugs that I got in Vaud. They say they break the sound and many get ear-trouble later from noise—I had not thought of that before."[62] This alternative dimension of silence, into which the ear-plugs remove the narrator, offers relief at a cost; it distances her from living in the war, from the immediacy of experience. The words and the noise weave a spell crucial to her identity as a writer: words keep her alive.

These stories also address specific realities of life during the Blitz: blue light bulbs, blackouts, countryside retreats, bombed warehouses, the restaurant Tea Kettle, sirens, and politicians. "Blue Lights" centers on a symbol evocative of the Blitz, the blue light bulbs that replaced regular bulbs during the blackouts; thus, blue lights for H.D. are something tangible as well as a state of mind. Blue bulbs emit minimal light, and combined with the black paper on the windows early in the war and then the later blackout curtains, they helped London disappear during the nighttime raids. Light was carefully policed because it drew bombers like beacons. Not only were homes dark, but the streets were also kept dark, which meant moving around after the blackout time was risky; there was no light to illuminate hazards blocking one's way and little medical treatment available for injuries. The blackout effectively kept H.D. and Bryher, and many other people, in their homes at night, as Bryher shared with Jordan: "The black out frightens me so much. It is such an awful feeling not to know if you are on the sidewalk or not, I never go out at night if I can help it."[63] H.D. and Bryher shared stories of London with Moore, and Moore commented on their astonishing depictions of the blackout and people sleeping in the subway tunnels.[64] Thousands of people were choosing to spend nights in the tunnels, which could provide more protection against bombs than their homes. Photographs show families in neat rows, sleeping not in comfort but in safety, night after night during the Blitz. A letter from Bryher to Howard reiterates their determination to avoid traveling during the blackout hours: "If it should be that you do have to experience raids, we found here that it was better to go on as if nothing had happened, except that we never went out if we could possibly avoid it, in the black out. To go out into the darkness merely uses up energy for nothing as a rule."[65]

Instead of hiding in subway tunnels, some people chose to leave London for the countryside, which was perceived as safer, and H.D. was often urged to retreat to Herring's newly rented home in Eckington. "Blue Lights" references the bright yellow canaries he found there, left behind by an owner who probably could no longer find food for them, a common problem for pet owners during the war. Herring, more resourceful than most, was determined to keep these colorful birds, symbols of better times, alive, and Moore responded by sending him birdseed.

"Warehouse" is based upon H.D. and Bryher's salvaging foray in Battersea, a London district across the Thames from H.D.'s neighborhood. Bryher's parents both passed away in the 1930s, and she stored items inherited from them in a warehouse, which was subsequently bombed. What they salvaged was delivered to the large, if temporary, home Herring was renting in the mining village of Eckington: "Mr. Herring has with great kindness offered to house the things (they were not many for all the furniture passed to my brother) that my mother left and that were damaged by water, after incendiaries hit the warehouse. Fortunately, the chief damage done was to the trunks."[66] Bryher likens Herring's house to a mansion on a reduced scale, akin to her wealthy parents' home on South Audley Street in London or Osbert and Edith Sitwell's mansion, Renishaw: "Only Bud's [Herring's] cottage is a mansion—a vast house like my Aunt's was, in Birmingham, almost a baby Audley for which he pays thirty shillings a week, merely because it happens to be in a sort of mining village. Everywhere very comfortable and very warm but one dresses for dinner—in other woollies! One does all the Renishaw things in miniature."[67]

Herring's home in Eckington housed *Life and Letters Today* after its premises in London were bombed, and it provided refuge to Herring's London friends who sought relief from the constant bombing. H.D. explained to her cousin, "I hope to stay on here though I am being urged to go to Eckington, near the Sitwells' beautiful old place, where friends have a house. Bryher has sent a number of her mother's things there, to help furnish the house and to keep them safe."[68] Retaining a sense of humor despite the hardships, Bryher and Herring "thought it would be funny to use up family stuff, impossible (but 'good') pictures, several impressive clocks, some very nice old chairs and desks and so on—family silver."[69] Bryher comments to H.D. that the effect is not quite what she had hoped: "Unfortunately this being a mansion the joke pictures are not suitable. At least Bud has hung them on stairs . . . but I think in a way they spoil the chaste effect of the other rooms."[70] "Warehouse" is bittersweet: the urgency of salvaging family items mingles with the sense that the pictures are "second-rate" and the memories of parents who purchased the paintings (125). The story ends with a return to the theme of time. H.D. has agreed to take a clock, a symbol of something old that needs repair but yet may survive to measure a new time, postwar time, if London can survive.

In "The Last Day," H.D. lunches with "Jo," her friend Silvia Dobson, who became a Land Girl, covered later in this introduction. Dobson's fictional name stemmed from H.D.'s assessment of her and her three sisters: "Funny girls these are not snapped up & decorative . . . but rather endearing; there were 4 Dobson girls; Ethne was killed on active service (air) and Molly, the other WREN is away on duty. Silvia, my little pal is the farmer & Nora keeps house & it is too 'Little Women' for words."[71] (Their brother also fought for Britain.) The restaurant where they have lunch is the Tea Kettle, H.D.'s neighborhood restaurant where she typically ate lunch. It was run by Miss Venables and Miss Docker, who worked hard to establish their restaurant and keep it running in the face of increasing difficulties: little food to offer patrons and few patrons to purchase it. In *The Days of Mars*, Bryher offers a description: "Up to 1941, its owners, Selina and Angelina, supplied their clients with soup, meat, two veg and dessert for two shillings and ninepence. They were country people, they bought all the ingredients they could directly from farms and the cooking was plain but excellent. . . . Up to the time that the restaurant was badly damaged by a bomb, Selina saw that our food was as honest as possible and not composed completely from powders."[72] Perdita also describes their resilience: "'Morning coffee, lunches and teas as usual unless a bomb falls on the build[ing].' So read the notice at H.D.'s local restaurant, The Tea Kettle. Then, one morning: 'more open than usual.' The waitresses were still sweeping up broken glass. And they were very apologetic. 'Sorry, only cold cuts and salad today, we seem to have lost our gas main.' They provided good scalding tea, however—brewed on a camping stove. Life had to go on, and so it did; cheerfully and sometimes grumpily—unless and until a bomb fell on the building."[73] This restaurant, like many others run by middle-class entrepreneurs, became a war casualty and subsequently the subject of Bryher's book *Beowulf*, a story of the women who ran this restaurant and their customers, ordinary civilians affected by World War II. Even an outing to this restaurant had its peril; Dobson describes one close shave: "Once, walking with Cat [H.D.] and Bryher to lunch at the Tea Kettle restaurant a dog fight happened overhead and bombs plummeted close to us. We stood still, very close together, knowing the futility of flight. The raider had already dumped his load and got away."[74]

Sirens plague the narrator in "Nefert" because they warn of incoming air raids, one more dangerous night.[75] Beginning in September 1939, the sirens became a constant during the Blitz, interrupting both sleep and the daytime, although eventually Londoners stopped taking notice. H.D. shared an anecdote about them with Francis Wolle: "Several times, I was in cinemas when there were warnings; the proprietor, usually in an old sweater and slacks would appear before the curtain and say, 'well, you all know why I'm here' and then there would be applause and he would pop back again. It was a regulation that there must be an official announcement, though of course the audience always heard the sirens or the gun-fire. Sometimes, the announcer would say in a bored voice, 'well, it's that man again.'"[76] The mournful cry of the Carter air-raid siren foreshadowed destruction, the destruction caused by at least 300 raids by April 1941, the date of this story. The narrator ponders the ways of death: "will I be burnt to death? will I suffocate? will I fall through my own floor? will my own wall fall on me?" She concludes "the nightmare is outside" (129).

"Saint Anthony" revolves around H.D.'s knowledge of politics, again underscoring her political acumen and the extent to which she engaged the politics of her time. H.D. knew the distinguished Anthony Eden only by reputation. Eden entered politics in 1923 as a Conservative member of Parliament and opposed the policy of appeasement in the late 1930s, resigning over Chamberlain's policies. By 1941 he was the secretary of state for foreign affairs, and Churchill recommended him as a successor should he be killed. Eden went on to serve as foreign secretary at three different times and became prime minister in 1955, serving until 1957 when his Middle East policy failed. In her story, H.D. recognizes him as an important person, a busy man, and she connects him to an Anthony for whom, years before, she had lit a candle in the Kapuzinerkirche, the Capuchin Church in Vienna, located in Neuer Market Square in the center of the city. It is a small church, famous for its central location and the Imperial Crypt, which houses the bodies of members of the Habsburg dynasty. H.D. confided to Jordan that while "I am not a conventional church-goer . . . I love popping in and out of old churches provided I am not CAUGHT there."[77] Moravianism, Catholicism, Buddhism, rosaries, candles, and politics intertwine as prayers of hope rise.

"Bunny"—the first of four stories that receive extended attention here—addresses the work that women were doing during the war, driving ambulances or mobile canteens, or serving as fire watchers. "The girl," based closely on Perdita, is driving into the bombed-out parts of London in a mobile canteen to feed the workers, especially Pioneers (a combat division used for light engineering tasks) and firefighters, involved in the clean-up effort, which allows her past the "no admission" signs marking areas where demolition squads work (109). She is joined on this one day by Bunny Thunder, an ambulance driver who incongruously wears blue pants and shoves her curly hair under a hat. Bunny refuses to take a night off because she might miss some of the action and during this day volunteered to drive the mobile canteen. Impressed with their fearless attitude, the narrator wonders if "these child Valkyries need anything of their somewhat astonished and not a little shattered mothers" (109).

Bunny Thunder is based on an actual woman by the same name about whom Perdita writes in her anonymous article in *Life and Letters Today*— the second piece in "Canteen Backstage"—which describes her experiences working for the Women's Voluntary Service (WVS) driving a mobile canteen during the winter of 1940–41.[78] At the beginning of the war, Perdita was working for *Life and Letters Today*, but when the journal relocated, she sought to contribute directly to the war effort. She first thought of volunteering as an Air Raid Protection (ARP) girl, but the ARP was already flooded with volunteers.[79] H.D. explained to Howard: "It is shocking to realize that, had she been a boy, he would already be called up. Her friends are busy in the army or in fire-stations, the A.R.P. of course, is one of the main services of interest in London."[80] Instead, Perdita volunteered to drive for the WVS, an experience she wrote about in her unpublished memoir:

> I answered a call for mobile canteen drivers, meals on wheels for the rescue workers digging out casualties, alive or dead.
>
> There were two of us, a partner buddy and I. We worked out of a depot in the East End, loaded the van and sped over broken glass, through the ruins, and parked where we could.
>
> "Here come the ministering angels!"
>
> Wonderful burly Cockneys, full of jokey banter. They had to maintain some balance of cheer on that grisly job, or go mad. They were so grateful as we poured tea and distributed buns, helter skelter.
>
> We then collected the mugs—no Styrofoam or paper cups in those days—and raced back to wash up, load up for the next round.
>
> Back and forth and on to yet another site. Pork pies, sausage rolls,

and sandwiches for lunch, cakes at tea time. And back to base: do the dishes, mop the floor, scrub the van.

Rush hours on the Underground [were] complicated by crowds ensconced for a safe night, a vast sprawling picnic at the bottom of a tunnel.[81]

Perdita's *Life and Letters Today* article similarly offered a window into one day of a WVS driver. When Perdita arrived at the WVS Center, the staff were helping people who had been bombed out of their homes find clothing and solace, and they were already feeding police officers and firefighters just off the night shift. Perdita readied the van: ninety-six white mugs, urns full of scalding water, cake, and Hershey's cocoa supplied by the American Red Cross. On this morning, the actual Bunny Thunder, "an extremely pretty girl in a tin hat and blue L.A.A.S. [London Area Ambulance Service] trousers," arrived to assist. Originally from Ireland, Bunny described her beloved job:

> "It's a bit hectic sometimes, when they're dropping lots of high explo-sives, but I wouldn't miss it for the world," she says. "I'm driving along, and suddenly a bomb whistles down. Will she take it, I wonder? The whole ambulance goes rocking from side to side, and I cling to the wheel, but she does stay the course, and I skirt the crater and drive on. One of our girls had the roof blown off her car, but she got her casual-ties to hospital on time."

Bunny drove the cantankerous van, which was largely without a second gear, through London, avoiding bombed-out streets and partial ruins being brought down with dynamite. They delivered cocoa, tea (with milk but little sugar), and cake so tough cutting it was "like sawing branches" to cold and hungry Pioneers, one lot after another until their supplies ran out. On her own for the afternoon, Perdita negotiated the debris-filled streets, waited for a building to fall, and scooted ahead of traffic with her "Priority" label. She fed the Canadian regiment, who thought they were going to London to fight but found themselves doing hard labor in the streets, and she served "dozens of teas, dozens of cakes" to anyone in khaki before returning to the Centre to prepare for tomorrow's repeat performance.[82]

After her stint with the mobile canteen, working in the most damaged parts of London during the worst fires, Perdita prepared to go to Leeds, where she would be trained to drive an ambulance in an American ambu-lance unit. H.D. described Perdita's plans to her American friends, writing that "I prefer it, to this town work, as the work will be more regular and she will be in a group and better looked after, I feel."[83] However, Perdita did not end up training to drive an ambulance, perhaps because of doctor's orders. H.D. wrote about Perdita's war activities that "eventually the doctor ordered her to find lighter work and she took a post under the government where her knowledge of foreign languages could be used. She has been cold, tired, uncomfortable, possibly even frightened though she never admitted this, but never did she question for a moment that any other course was possible."[84]

Perdita first worked for the British government, using the formidable language skills learned during her childhood in Switzerland and continental travels—which unfortunately included little Italian, and Perdita commented that early on she could only recognize "one word, 'Perdita' which keeps on occurring"[85]—and the change agreed with her, in part because government workers were fed better than the general populace: "She looks ever so well, was much gayer, as her present billets are very comfortable, she gets lots of milk and eggs and she is terribly amused with her bicycle. Also they have a new cook and better food where she works. But . . . this is too gloriously tapeworm and hush hush, she had to work on Italian which she never learnt. Don't ask why."[86] In 1943, Pearson offered Perdita a chance to work with his unit; he was in Britain as part of the American Office of Strategic Services (OSS): "I wish I might tell you and her more about the nature of the work we do. But she may be sure that it is fascinating to me, at least. And that I am interested in her simply because her qualifications do seem to me to fit her for the work. I find it both curious and pleasing that my questions about your daughter may lead to filling a gap in our office."[87] Perdita took the job: "The work is interesting . . . very pleasant & fun & the girls are a very snapped up, decorative bunch. It seems to be even more hush-hush than the previous phase of my career, which is a great bore as I should so like to tell the world. However, it *is* fun."[88] Although she never shared many details about this work, Perdita worked as a translator and code breaker for the OSS, the precursor to the CIA.[89]

The same "type" as Bunny, Goldie appears in the poem "May 1943" in *What Do I Love?* A driver of an emergency car—an ambulance or mobile canteen—Goldie was warned that the fires were getting hot, but "Goldie wouldn't move away, / she was told to stay." After being found "sitting upright / at the wheel of her emergency car, / dead," Goldie briefly makes the paper; just a photograph and a caption commemorate her life, one casualty of many (160). H.D. chose her as a central figure of this poem because she represents the stubborn British spirit in its willingness to sacrifice. As the Americans entered the war and began experiencing its hardships, they chafed over the rationing and shortages, realities the British had been living with for years. The British nation, for which H.D. uses the metaphor of a ship,[90] perseveres because the people refuse to leave or give up; they refuse to flee as rats do in the cliché: "the ship didn't sink / because / the rats knew / the timber true" (162). Goldie's final sacrifice, common in people her age, represents the national spirit.

H.D.'s voracious reading about the war included *Swastika Nights* by Katharine Burdekin, who was then using the pseudonym Murray Constantine. This 1937 dystopia envisions a world devastated by seven centuries of Nazi rule. Women have been reduced to the level of breeding animals and are housed in a caged part of town reserved for male sexual release and the production of male children. Men are hierarchically organized into the dominated nations, the regular male Nazis, and the ruling Knights, one of whose family has carefully preserved a book—all others having been destroyed—that documents a partial history of the world reaching back beyond Nazi origins. This Knight understands that his world may end because the preference for male children has become so overwhelming that women are no longer birthing many girls, and he tentatively decides to sow knowledge and insurrection by sharing the book with others. However, his chosen heir dies at novel's end, so while change is still possible, it is not probable. This cautionary tale is remarkably feminist and speaks to the Nazi predilection to dominate women entirely. It draws a dismal portrait of what a world dedicated to such a perverted masculinity would mean for women.

A realistic book—a reminiscence, quasi-diary—H.D. also recommended to her friends was the 1938 *With Malice toward Some* by Margaret Halsey, in which Halsey continually points out that a woman's position in England was much more restricted than a man's. In this hilariously ironic book observing England from the point of a visiting American woman—which H.D. enjoyed even though she felt she was probably given it by accident, it not being the type of literature she typically went in for—the narrator comments that "I felt rather cast down at listening to Henry's report, for it made me realize how little point there is in a woman's keeping a diary in a country where the best food, the best clothes, the best clubs, the best conversation and practically all the liquor are for men."[91] Halsey's laments and Burdekin's dystopia are countered in "Bunny," which envisions a much more open future for women.

H.D. ends "Bunny" with one of the most feminist statements in all of her texts—and one inexplicably excised from the 1993 publication of this story.

She imagines watching the young women as they work in the most dangerous areas of London:

> ... they stride across barriers, marked clear for all to read, no admis-
> sion, dangerous, land-mine or time-bomb or just demolition squad and
> dynamite.
>
> They are pushing out the borders, they enter the inner rim, not in
> any "feminine rights" manner, but in some heroic way that has nothing
> to do with their blue pants, they take them pretty much for granted.
> The blue pants and those pretty legs, they walk in and through the
> flames, they have crossed the circle. Outside in life, every day, all day, in
> the black night, all night, those pretty feet are pushing forward in a new
> dance, a cosmic dance of heroism, such as the world has never seen nor
> dreamed of. (110)

Herring agrees with her assessment that this war has fundamentally changed
the world for women: "As to coming back, it's uncertain to what. It's quite
certain it won't be the Old Home for the Old Life. We have seen to it that we
have scuttled that more than we knew. The women won't be there to come
back to. That is to say, both men's and women's idea of Woman will have
changed."[92] H.D. herself lived the generation that bridged the True Woman
ideal to the New Woman, cutting her hair, shortening her skirts, smoking
cigarettes on the street. Admiringly, she watches her daughter—whom she
describes as "so gay and brave"—"in the swing and vibration of her own generation" further extend the boundaries of what is allowed for women.[93]

Into her story "Escape" H.D. weaves not people she knew but the plot of
the film Escape. Upon exiting the theater, the narrator in "Escape" finds herself wading into a fresh snowstorm and a new barrage of bombs exploding
over London; the film's story segued too smoothly into her real life. Released
November 1, 1940, the film follows the character Mark Preysing to Germany
to find his mother, Emmy Ritter, who is being held in a concentration camp
and has been sentenced to death as a traitor. Her obscure crime seems to
be transferring money from the sale of her father's house out of Germany
and then speaking out against oppression at her trial. The film juxtaposes
romance—Mark falls in love with the Countess Ruby von Treck, born an
American and now a German widow with a Nazi general for a lover—with
a portrayal of the oppressive German nation through the fear of ordinary
Germans to cross their government, the brutality of the German courts, and
the military complex later to be known as the Bergen-Belsen concentration

camp. The townspeople balk at helping Mark out of fear for their own safety until Dr. Berthold Ditten, a doctor at the camp, meets him unexpectedly over a drink and the next day gives Emmy a dose of a drug that simulates death. With help from a reluctant family friend and the countess, who has now fallen in love with him, Mark revives his mother and escapes with her on a flight to the United States. The countess, at the last moment, refuses to accompany him and stalls the German pursuit by taunting her lover, General Kurt von Kolb, with her new feelings for Mark, causing the general's weak heart to fail. Having saved her new American friends, the countess is left in Germany to face an uncertain future, but her courage—she was born an American, after all, the film reinforces—redeems the town.

In H.D.'s story "Escape," the narrator comments that German brutality and the concentration camps had been known to her and her friends for many years, but other people in Britain are shocked by the stories then being revealed in the newspapers. She offers a quotation from *J'Accuse!*, a sixty-page document published by the World Alliance for Combating Anti-Semitism in 1933 whose title is borrowed from Emile Zola's 1898 letter accusing the French government of anti-Semitism in the case of Alfred Dreyfus. Robert Herring sent *J'Accuse!* to Bryher, who shared it with H.D.[94] This document delineates Nazi attacks against German Jews, like an attack on Ezriel Weiss, who was kidnapped at gunpoint, beaten, and robbed of his passport and a ring; Issac Adler, who was beaten and his shop windows destroyed; Joel Zisapel, his wife, and son, who were beaten "till they were a mass of blood" and robbed of 3,200 marks and various goods—an extensive list of horrific crimes of which the Hollywood *Escape* seems almost a parody.[95] By the time *Escape* was appearing in theaters, H.D. and her circle had been familiar with German crimes for at least seven years, years during which the world purposefully ignored the evidence repeatedly offered. H.D. wrote to Jordan that "Br[yher] and I were all very much 'in' it, on the continent, long before people became aware here—Br[yher] you know—did a lot of rescue work for Jews and non-Jews who had sympathies etc.—many of them exceptionally gifted people from the universities—Vienna, Prague etc."[96] Bryher tells Moore that "There is absolutely NOTHING and I don't want to boast that I don't know about refugees in Europe!"[97]

H.D. and Jordan were friends with Ezra Pound in their youth; both were disturbed by his Fascist biases and corresponded about his activities on the international stage. H.D. describes a friend's impressions of his broadcasts as "too, too terrible, illiterate and dull," and she writes Jordan that "Ezra was reputed in pre-war Paris to be doing actual [Fascist] propaganda, so that every letter he writes, he runs down Jews, it's tiresome but I believe is part of his 'job' if he is a job [*sic*]—it sounds horrid and I may malign him but people in Paris said he was working definitely for the Italian dictator." Writing that Pound is "making such a clown of himself," H.D. shares her long-standing misgivings: "Also E[zra] tried to get my daughter in touch with some pro-fascist friends of his—that was before the war but I was already very well-aware of what might be going to happen and did not like the idea of P[erdita] being exploited—it was not QUITE as crude as that but that is what it looked like."[98]

In contrast to her feelings about Pound, H.D. was particularly worried about Sylvia Beach, who chose to stay in France during the war. Bryher described Beach, a member of their intimate circle:

> She had a very famous bookshop in Paris where all the Americans went, who were studying at the Sorbonne, she arranged for lectures and meetings and introductions for them and helped the French who wanted to read American books. Her father was at the American church in Paris years ago, then moved to Princeton but he is very elderly and retired long ago. Sylvia was the type of person who is the highest type of citizen . . . very gay but always so anxious to help and explain and with a tremendous feeling of responsibility. I have been so worried about her. She would not leave Paris because she said she might be able to help.[99]

An American in occupied France and therefore an enemy of the state, Beach was interned in Vittel from August 1942 to February 1943, a difficult experience she writes rather light-heartedly about in "Inturned."[100] She remained very much on H.D.'s and Bryher's minds until they finally hear from her in 1944.

Films, "Escape" implies, create a fictitious world into which one should be able to enter and exit through the door of the theater, but in this case, the film *Escape* overlaps with the real London. The film, set in northern Germany, offers snow-covered landscapes, and at the very moment of the story, London is enjoying a rare snow, into which the narrator steps. The newsreel brings real war news into the theater while simultaneously the snow transforms London into a film set. Snow muffles traffic sound and amplifies voices, creating an all-encompassing studio out of the real world. Even though there has been no warning siren, bombs begin to fall in London, matching the gunfire in the newsreels. Fortuitously hopping in a cab, the narrator inhabits a war scene similar to the one she just viewed, in which her cab driver jokes with another about the possibility of being hit by a bomb—the unreality of their reality. In the same miraculous way Emmy Ritter is delivered from execution by the Nazis, H.D. hopes for escape from the Blitz.

Time and the role of the writer return in "The Ghost," which takes place at the Sitwells' estate, Renishaw. The Sitwell family traced itself back to royalty, the Plantagenets, Robert Bruce, and the Macbeths; it had owned the opulent Renishaw Hall since the seventeenth century; and Sir George and Lady Ida Sitwell bore three children: Edith, Osbert, and Sacheverell Sitwell. All three were gifted writers, well known to their contemporaries and influential in London's literary scene for their poetry, their literary parties, and their aristocratic flamboyance. H.D. had been acquainted with the Sitwells since the 1910s through her then husband Richard Aldington; Bryher wrote Moore that she had known Edith since 1925;[101] and Osbert wrote Bryher fond letters dating from the 1930s onward, but they all became particularly close during World War II. Perdita describes their friendship:

The Sitwells, the three of them—Edith, Osbert, and Sacheverell, known as Sashie—and my mother, the poet H.D., and her lifelong companion Bryher had all known each other over the years, as cordial acquaintances. The war brought about the true meeting of minds. Restless travelers grounded on our small beleaguered island. Ardent creative spirits determined to rise above the dreariness and weariness and intermittent terrors of those times. Sashie was no longer an immediate member of the triumvirate. He had a life of his own, as country squire with his beautiful wife Georgia and their two sons.

"Like the uncle of a king," is how Gertrude Stein described Osbert. Patrician, infinitely kind, courteous, elegantly understated. "Very tiresome" was his only comment on a night of bombing that had nearly blown him from his home. He and Bryher became the very closest of friends. They met every morning for a walk in Hyde Park. They exchanged long letters when separated, even wrote to each other when both were in town—afterthoughts on their earlier conversations.

Edith was anything but understated. She never faced the world until late afternoon, yet she seemed ever present through telephone calls and letters. She'd finished a poem or couldn't finish it. Her throat had flared up again, her lumbago was killing her, insomnia was driving her to the brink of madness. My mother retreated from these little dramas. Bryher loved them and would go rushing off bearing cough syrup, liniment, reference books from the London Library."[102]

Bryher summed up her feelings: "I sometimes wonder whether I should have survived the war if it had not been for Osbert's friendship and Edith's love."[103]

During the war, their parents having passed away, Edith and Osbert returned to Renishaw, which they offered as a refuge to their many friends. Renishaw's famed gardens were much diminished by the war, when cabbages needed to be grown instead of roses, but Bryher wrote to Moore in 1941 that "I wish you could see Renishaw—it is of an entrancing beauty and to-day they had had a gift of orchids from a famous garden where, due to the war, stocks had had to be reduced."[104] Bryher visited Renishaw often, and H.D. did on occasion.

"The Ghost" turns on a spring visit in 1941, possibly March 21 because that was the first day of spring, the fête-day, according to the character based on Osbert referred to simply as "he," when the garden statuary was unveiled for the season. Edith wrote to Bryher about a spring visit by H.D., perhaps the one commemorated in the story: "I lunched with H.D. & Robert [Herring] yesterday, and thought H.D. looked really better. In fact, I would hardly have known her, for one thing, her eyes have lost that look of needing to *bleed*. Poor thing, *how* ill she looked when she arrived first."[105] Renishaw with its art, gardens, and peace may indeed have cured H.D. of the look of "needing to bleed." In "The Ghost," the narrator is awed by her surroundings: the furnishings, the art, the statues, the paintings. When admiring the paintings, she remarks that she prefers the pink youth. Pleased, "he" replied, "that is the ghost," to reinforce both the aristocracy of his ancient home—naturally there would be a ghost—and her artist's insight as she is able to see the ghost just as she has seen into the fourth dimension in other stories (144).

The clocks themselves in this story lie because they have been pushed ahead by two hours. Daylight saving time was adopted year-round during World War II to save energy, and the clocks were set ahead yet another hour in the summer to extend the evenings and save even more energy. H.D. explained it to Jordan: "We are two hours here ahead of the clock—it is called double summer-time and I can't say that I am yet used to the extra hour; it came on about a week ago. Now nearing seven and supper time, it is really 5 and tea-time, rather like Alice in Wonderland. Some people say they simply go by the clock but being sensitive to day and night, I can't seem to re-adjust."[106] Bryher enjoyed the long evenings offered by double summer time, but she agreed that it felt odd to eat an eight o'clock breakfast at six.[107] Time works in unexpected ways, according to the story, years making patterns as well as marking the passage of time. Time can be a spiral, a nautilus shell; it can shimmer like mercury; it can cause a metamorphosis. It repeats itself: there was another, earlier, war, other Germans—but this is the war that will determine the future of Britain and of art.

The future of art is being determined by this war because a younger generation of writers has arrived on the scene who accuse H.D.'s generation of being escapists. The narrator responds, "How many blitz-nights, did you spend in London? This was poor pride" (141). Poor pride though it might be, this one sentence reaches into the heart of the matter—can one be out of touch if living in the midst of the fire and bombing? This sentence reasserts the primacy of the modernists; this war is not demonstrating that their generation is outdated but that their literary careers have been broken across by a constant cycle of war. World War II facilitates H.D.'s epics *Trilogy* and *Helen in Egypt*; she had not written such extended lyrical sequences before this war, and many of her contemporaries also produced epics as mature artists at the height of their powers: Langston Hughes's *Montage of a Dream Deferred*, William Carlos Williams's *Patterson*, T. S. Eliot's *Four Quartets*, Ezra Pound's *Cantos*, even Marianne Moore's *Collected Poems*.

Although H.D. was not friends with Virginia Woolf, they certainly knew of each other, and H.D. owned and read Woolf's books. She introduces the question of Woolf's suicide here: "The late Mrs. Woolf who walked into a river, but a few weeks ago, was real. She was real. Her death was a sign of failure, or not? Having done her work, one camp protested, she was well out of it. Had she done her work?" (141). This attitude implies that if Woolf had indeed done her work, then escaping the war is a practical choice. When H.D. falls ill in 1946, Dobson frets about her because of precisely this attitude; she writes that H.D. said to her about Woolf's suicide that "[Woolf] had a perfect right to take her own life."[108] In a May 1941 letter to May Sarton, H.D. wrote about Woolf's suicide:

> Virginia W. was a great shock to us all. I am glad you say it seemed "unnecessary," as that is JUST how I felt and feel. The general attitude was "poor thing—she went through such a lot—" but having been through so much, I myself, did feel stricken to think she got away like that, just when really everything is very exciting and one longs to be able to live to see all the things that will be bound to happen later—think of not being here to look at France, to watch the whole shift of this civilization. Times were NEVER so exciting—the last war was not. It is simply a sheer mathematical problem of HOW much can the human frame

stand and endure—and we seem to get stronger, as far as nerves go, as we go on. That is, people who left early can not stand it at all, but those who stuck it, are very blithe and chirpy, except for individual losses and frets, there is so little defeatism. . . . Virginia's body was found in the river as expected. There was inquest and letter left to her husband, she believed she was going mad again and could not face it. One heard "poor Ophelia" . . . but, like you, I did not think it the right end somehow, no matter how poetical and traditional.[109]

Written in 1941, this letter reflects the chin-up British attitude H.D. had internalized even though the worst hardships of the war had not yet been realized. The war, on some levels, energized H.D., and it certainly engendered some of her very best writing. She seemed to find Woolf's suicide a disappointment. If, as the Osbert character voices, circumstances created by war like famine shape the "actual aesthetic ideas of nations," then H.D. expects her generation to be key players in producing the new art in the new world (144). She offers no sense that her creative days are over.

The final story of this collection, "Before the Battle," was written first, during the summer of 1940 as the Battle of Britain began, but H.D. found it a fitting conclusion because, she wrote, it "acts as an introduction to the selection of poems *What Do I Love*."[110] The narrator is trying to sleep during the early bombings, and she particularly worries about whether Russia will support Britain or not. (This question remained undetermined until June 1941 when Germany attacked the Soviet Union and Stalin signed a mutual assistance treaty with Britain.) She lies and sweats, reciting Psalm 23 in the "cosmic tidewaves of terror" (145). Her daughter, lovely in a flowered dress and blue hair ribbon, unexpectedly appears at the door, a tender image juxtaposed with the terrors of the night. Her daughter wants to talk about her newly penned autobiography *Pre-war*, which her friend Jack designates as selfish, since it is about herself rather than the current war. His rejection of her work drives her to the comfort of her mother's flat, where her supportive mother suggests that he might be jealous of her work. However much her book worries her mother, she defends her daughter, as they negotiate the shifting space between parent and grown child. As the daughter leaves, going back into the blackout to her own flat, the story moves to Bethlehem, Pennsylvania, where H.D. was born, now becoming a story about the narrator and her own mother.

The daughter's book, here titled *Pre-war*, is Perdita's *Autobiography*, which exists in manuscript form in H.D.'s papers at the Beinecke Rare Book and Manuscript Library at Yale University. It is a story of Perdita's life before World War II, one of Perdita's youthful efforts to find her way. Growing up in a family of writers, writing a book seemed logical. Perdita knew many of the famous literary figures of her day; she had lived an adventurous and unconventional life; and at age twenty, she had more material upon which to draw than most people. Unfortunately, her book described real events and people from her life, and while H.D. wrote autobiographical texts herself, she loathed the thought of "a few H.D.s" being placed "like cherries on the cock-tails of Desmond and Co," Perdita's ill-chosen suitor.[111] As the daughter of H.D. and Bryher, Perdita was a wealthy woman, and her mothers worried that the men dating her were after her fortune. (It is suggested that she may have made a will in a young man's favor at one point.) Perdita painstakingly wrote her autobiography—it was so long that Macpherson termed it an "epic"[112]—she retyped it herself, wrote family friends like Moore about it, and was planning to send it to publishers. H.D. worried about its contents, even while she admired her daughter's tenacity: "I must say Pup's book has been a shock to us all, and it is a good thing, but I don't want her to START on the [Robert] McAlmon level of back-chat about us all." She asked Macpherson, who was reading the book for Perdita, to stall it and to convince her of the wisdom of using pseudonyms for its characters. Walter Schmideberg suggested that its chances of publication were slim, given the paper shortage.[113] In response, Bryher suggests that it could be published in the United States: "I should not worry too much about Pup's [Perdita's] book, the young are apt to do such things, why not if she would alter names a bit, get her to get it out rather au States. Nobody would know there what it was all supposed to be."[114] H.D. herself was careful not to use real names in her texts. For example, in the carbon copy of "Warehouse," Bryher's name is scratched out and replaced with "Bee."

After Perdita drove a mobile canteen and planned to take an ambulance course, she even considered running a nightclub. In response to one of her schemes, Bryher wrote to H.D., "Now don't let that wretched Pup upset you—Buddy [Herring] giggled and I simply feel well, if she wants to be such an idiot, let her get on with it and get it over."[115] Bryher, a financial whiz, had structured Perdita's capital so that it could not be touched; Perdita could only spend her income, and if she squandered it, she might learn a valuable lesson, they thought. Once ensconced in government work using her languages, Perdita's escapades died down, and H.D. was pleased that Perdita did not marry "her very, very distinctly Mr. Wrong."[116] Once the war ended, Perdita moved to New York, took some classes, and became engaged to the book publisher for whom she was working as a secretary. In 1950, Perdita announced her engagement and impending wedding, and H.D. and Bryher approved of her choice. H.D. wrote to Perdita, "I am really so happy and I do feel that you know your own mind and interests and what is more important, emotions and HEART. Be sure, we will rejoice in your happiness and feel blessed in it."[117] Bryher's words to H.D. are equally touching: "We simply don't have to worry any more. She has found what she wanted."[118]

Perdita's happiness and safety were paramount to H.D. Their relationship has been rendered many ways, some of which paint H.D. as an unloving or disconnected mother because she allowed Bryher to adopt Perdita; she used child care; she protected her writing time; she traveled without her daughter in tow; she did not fuss or gush. However, it is important that the depth of H.D.'s love for Perdita be recognized, even if her parenting choices jar some expectations. Perdita kept a box of intimate correspondence from her mother, letters which she did not deposit at the Beinecke and which her family still treasures. These exceptionally sweet letters articulate the depth of H.D.'s love for her daughter and the importance to H.D. of their relationship. For example, a letter written to Perdita on the occasion of her marriage reads, "What C A N I say but I L O V E Y O U and bless you and think of you two blessed and happy together."[119] *What Do I Love?* is published the same year Perdita marries, perhaps a happy coincidence, perhaps for what H.D. did love.

"Before the Battle" concludes on a hopeful note, reflecting on H.D.'s mother and her childhood in the Moravian culture, as well as her present life in London with her own daughter: "I am safe now. We built a great fire, brought back a dead log to life, we got warm, she and I together brought back the spring" (151). Both mother/daughter pairs are figured as Persephone and Demeter, and their reunion brings the spring, a time of renewal. Several other stories in this collection have equally positive messages. In "She Is Dead," a dream vision leads the narrator to conclude that part of herself has died, decimated by the war, and she witnesses a funeral. This figurative death represents a part of her that was already dead but not yet relinquished, and that death leads to a wedding and new life. As a writer, shedding this self allows her to write in new ways; she is no longer defined by the "stalactite-shaped running verse that, on a page, looked broken, a stalactite with the ridges and furrows, frozen" (132). Rebirth is also a theme in "The Last Day," which ends with "a dream of peace and hope. It seems to indicate that though our houses and our minds have been sliced open by the attacks of the enemy overhead, that, overhead is as well, the great drift of stars, and those stars found entrance into the shattered house of life" (128). Despite the devastation wreaked on London, minds have been opened to the future, as houses have been sliced open by the bombs. "Before the Battle" ends with the line "This war is over, I tell you," a wishful sentiment in 1940, but one that H.D. later reads as prophetic and as an appropriate setting for the poems in *What Do I Love?* (151).

Right on the heels of *Within the Walls*, H.D. wrote a piece for the July 1941 *Bryn Mawr Alumnae Bulletin* in which she addresses the naïveté of the Americans who still maintained that the war could be stopped rather than fought. Throughout the 1930s, the United States passed successive Neutrality Acts and resisted involvement in World War II. The official end of this policy came in March 1941 with the Lend-Lease Act, which allowed the United States to support nations by providing by sale, lending, or gift war materials. However, the United States was still not a full participant in the war effort until December 1941 when the Japanese attacked Pearl Harbor, after which the United States declared war on Japan, Germany and Italy declared war on the U.S., and the United States responded with its own war declaration. While decrying war in "A Letter from England," H.D. delineates her experiences in both the first war and into the second, arguing that England is all that stands between Germany and an eventual attack on the United States. She describes the solidarity of the people in London:

> As for myself, I was continuously in London from the day the blitz started until about a week ago when I came to the country for a short rest. It is the noise that is so trying, the many different sorts of explosions, the smell of dust and rubble and charred wood. I cannot say here that one thinks of the young as young, but somehow of everybody, from the old ladies of nearly seventy who smother incendiaries with sandbags, the patient workers of all ages, who may lose their homes during darkness but turn up punctually to work next day, the children my daughter knows who are working at rest centers, in the services, and on the land. It is a whole people and I think as united as any nation can ever hope to be[120]

Her testimony presents a strong front against the Nazis, and she argues that one must fight because "there is such a thing as morality and it has been impossible for us, who have perhaps still something of the Puritan in us, to bear what we have had to see here of the persecution of all intellectual thought by Fascism, unmoved."[121] This call to arms was meant to move her readers, educated and influential graduates of Bryn Mawr, out of isolation and into battle. She claimed that England's only sin might have been to enter the war too late, but otherwise, it is on the side of the angels and deserves the backing of Americans, who will be at risk themselves should England fall.

"Look Before You Sleep," ©Imperial War Museums (PST 0753).

Remain You Our Goddess of Raids

"Death was our constant companion," wrote Silvia Dobson, of 1941 and 1942, which she called the "worst years of World War II."[122] H.D. fairly assumed she might die in the war. She asked Moore to represent her literary interests in the United States, and Moore was clear when writing to one publisher: "I have been asked by H.D. to make author's decisions for her in this country during the war, and in case of her death to assume responsibility of her American published work."[123] H.D.'s first will on record dates from 1943, but three years earlier she wrote Bryher to specify that certain bequests be given to the owners of the Tea Kettle, cousins like Howard, and friends like Moore and that particular attention be paid to Perdita: "I am of course worried about Pup. You have been so gracious and heavenly to her and I suppose you will see what is best to be done. I do not mean to appear fatalistic, but at this time, it is wrong to leave anything unsaid."[124] In June, Germany attacked the Soviet Union, which consequently signed a mutual assistance treaty with Britain. H.D. was overjoyed by this development: "It is heavenly about Russia. Every hour will make a difference to us. You do not know what it means to feel the tide has turned, though I do not dare hope, we have seen the end of the air-raids."[125] Despite the good news, the air raids returned in July. In a letter to her American friend and fellow Bryn Mawr alumna Mary Herr, a librarian who sent H.D. American publications and food packages, H.D. wrote, "We had a lull of 11 whole weeks, then our 567th alarm or 'alert' as we call it, Sunday night about 2, and I must say after the heavenly peace, it was a shock to get back into all that. However, I am ready again, it was the surprise that upset me, it was not a serious raid. And we are all so happy about Russia and of course, have long been, about USA supplies. One leading article some weeks ago was headed

USA   USSR   and US

which is very illuminating, I think."[126] H.D. commented to Bryher that Perdita "was beginning to worry lest the guns had grown 'rusty.' She need have had no cause for alarm, on that score."[127] Once again, rain was welcomed as a deterrent to the Luftwaffe, curtains were drawn, and no end was in sight. When H.D. headed to Cornwall in August, Bryher listed the items she must be sure to bring: her gas mask (a test was scheduled for that week), her identity card, and her ration book.[128] The Blitz was over, but the years of perseverance had only begun.

In September 1941, H.D. was returning from six weeks in Cornwall when she met the RAF pilot about whom she wrote the second poem in *What Do I Love?* "R.A.F." All of Britain was aware of what it owed the RAF, and in June 1942, *Life and Letters Today* dedicated an issue to the men protecting Britain in the skies. Herring applauded: "they manipulate planes and guns single-handed, send the foe spinning in flames or may themselves be shot down, ablaze. They land planes riddled to skeletons, or bale out over the sea. They will engage in duels miles above the earth and come down, by parachute, in the middle of Weymouth High Street, narrowly—as did one pilot—to escape being run over by a bus."[129] He filled the issue with stories about the RAF's beginnings, the men supporting the pilots, a flyer's return home, and poems by service members. It was with some astonishment that H.D. found herself physically entwined with one of these glamorous flyers on a crowded train. In a September 18 letter to Bryher, H.D. described the encounter:

> Had a R.A.F. in our compartment, about 6 foot 3 or more; stuttered like the B. [Walter Schmideberg]; I was rather shattered as he sat opposite me in his corner and our very long legs though discreet seemed to approve of the others—when his wouldn't go anywhere, I suggested his putting them right up on my side; he refused of course, but when I seemed to doze off, there they were. It appears he is "resting," though he said, most emphatic, "but that doesn't prevent my flying." He has had some sort of operation, he said "operation," I thought he meant "operations" flight—didn't ask him what. I had a few minutes with him when the others went in to tea. I told him he wasn't English and he said he was Scotch but he said "I'm hanged if I see how you know that." I didn't KNOW it, I felt it. This upset me very much as I haven't been so near a R.A.F. peppered over with ribbons . . . and at that slept, which isn't meant to be bawdy but makes for intimacy when all 4 legs have no where to go.[130]

After writing the poem, H.D. mentioned it to May Sarton: "It is odd that I should be writing about the air too—a sort of abstract, personal tribute to a

RAF youth who crashed—part real, part imaginary, part symbolic, done in rather simple couplets and I do NOT know what it looks like but have to do it—as you say, one must create oneself and can only live that way—and the self and the poem are one."[131]

The poem begins in this encounter with the pilot's words "I'm just out of hospital / but I'm still flying." His eyes hold the passion of war, a

... white-heat,

all the fires of the wind,
fire of sleet,

snow like white-fire pellets,
congealed radium, planets

like snow-flakes (165)

The poem shifts to a dream sequence in which the pilot appears as a savior "from a far star," and the persona thanks him for his sacrifices in the Battle of Britain (166). He wears "the mark / of the new cross, / the flying shadow / of high wings," perhaps the RAF shoulder flash or badge, which both feature an eagle, wings outstretched, head lowered, eyeing his prey (168). The RAF motto "Per Ardua ad Astra" translates to "Through Struggle to the Stars," neatly fitting H.D.'s vision of the pilot as an emissary from the stars. In its final two sections, the poem shifts back to the train, where the real pilot, so very tall, cannot get comfortable, and the persona wedges his feet into the space left on her seat. He apologizes for inconveniencing her, and her gratitude for him and his fellow flyers lingers in the air, unspoken in the train but articulated forever in the poem: "I want / personally to thank you / for what you have done" (167).

During the fall of 1941, H.D. reassured American cousins and friends that she was still committed to remaining in London, now ordained as the capital of the free world, a beacon to occupied Europe, as claimed by Madeline Henrey in *The Incredible City*, which covers the first years of the war, another book H.D. recommended to others. Henrey describes Europeans desperately escaping the continent and finding themselves in London, a city critical to the imagination of an occupied Europe. Early in the war, shops in London still had cakes, flowers, and white bread, which had disappeared in other countries. London was an exciting, cosmopolitan city filled with refugees and troops from all parts of Europe: "The extent to which London had become the centre of the civilized world was continually evident. People from the farthest corners of the earth met others born in the same little spot as themselves, and such meetings often took place in Piccadilly Circus or Leicester Square."[132] London became a beacon for Europe, hope for a freed future: "The enemy thought he could wipe out the City in a night. He failed to do so. The City's agony wrote a glorious page in our nation's history." The incredible city in the book's title is London, a city with "the toughness of Sparta, the culture of Athens, and the adventurous spirit of Elizabethan times. The streets are full of men and women who have met adventure—airmen back from bombing raids, sailors from convoy, and soldiers from the bloodstained lemon groves of Southern Italy."[133] This city symbolized free Europe, and its existence, however tested by the enemy, offered hope. H.D. reassures Jordan that she is safe and unwilling to abandon a country from which she has "taken joy and comfort": "the Blitz last year was of course, very terrible, but if everyone had rushed away, there would have been, or might have been, the same trouble that there was in France. Anyhow, though the trough of the wave does, at times, seem to go right into inferno, the crest of the wave holds compensations."[134]

On December 7, 1941, the Japanese attacked Pearl Harbor, and the United States formally entered World War II in both the Pacific and European theaters. Two days later, H.D. wrote Herr that "I often envy you all, over there, but I should have been disturbed and restive, not to have been here, though I never thought that I or anyone could have absorbed so much bomb-shock and still live to tell the tale. . . . I listen constantly to the B.B.C., we have a 'London calling Europe' three times daily, which really makes me feel in touch with the continent, and French, German and Italian broadcasts daily from London, abroad, keep one up to scratch with one's languages; in fact, oddly the world has come to London."[135] Constantly looking to the future, H.D. wrote Howard that "I felt at the time of worst raids, that heightening of perception, only wanted to stick on to enjoy the after war days, and am immensely curious to see how the world will shape."[136]

Already the world was being reshaped with the conscription of women, which Herring saw as the most momentous change to the social order: "Raids, rationing (even 'points'), shortages and restrictions of all kinds we accept, with complaint or complaisance, but without great spiritual upheaval. We accustom ourselves to be numbers rather than names. We have prepared ourselves for uncongenial work, dull or dangerous duties, and enforced separations. These are changes to be expected and, recognized, the more easily to be endured. But there are other changes which cannot be recognized, because they are new to this war. The greatest of these is the conscription for women."[137] At the beginning of the war, H.D. commented in several letters that if Perdita were a man, she would already have been called up for duty, but soon the women were included.

In the 1942 *You and the Call-Up*, Robert S. W. Pollard synthesizes the various governmental decrees concerning compulsory service. In short, men and women between the ages of eighteen and fifty-one could be conscripted to work for the military, industry, and fire-watching.[138] Despite the many exceptions, including those for married women and women raising young children,[139] women were subject to much the same service as men. But even though the nation needed their service, Britain was still uncomfortable with women fighting, and so "no woman who is called up for military service under the Act is required actually to use any lethal weapon unless she has signified in writing her willingness to use lethal weapons or, as the case may be, to take part in the use thereof."[140] Women were not called up who were already working in occupations considered vital war work like the land army, medical care, and canteen workers.[141]

Bryher explained the conscription policies to Jordan: "I had to register along with the grandmothers but am reserved in my job, as I expected to be. It is all right for me, as I have been working the last twenty years but I do not think it right to call up women of fifty out of their homes. . . . I think they [Americans] don't realize that they make no distinction here but call up the women as they call up the men. You can be sent anywhere in England. And to any kind of work."[142] The government had indeed taken control over employment. People could be forced to work in activities needed for the war effort and even to live away from home (an exception allowed married women to remain with their families). Of particular interest to H.D. was the restriction that women between twenty and thirty years old, like Perdita, were prohibited from changing their employment except with permission from the Ministry of Labor so as to keep valuable employees in necessary occupations.[143]

In 1942 letters, H.D. repeatedly recommended the film *Mrs. Miniver* as an accurate portrait of Britain's war experiences. She tells her cousin Hattie Howard that she was "deeply touched and thrilled" by it and that while events are telescoped into 132 minutes, they ring true: "The capture of the German pilot for instance, has actually happened like that here—the first one I remember hearing about, was much on those lines, only in a way even more dramatic—I forget the woman's name but she simply found a pilot in the fields and ordered him to the house; of course, these men came down dazed and some said, doped, but there was much very simple and astonishingly competent action from ordinary unarmed people. The boats in the river on the way to Dunkirk, was so well done too."[144] *Mrs. Miniver* condensed what had become common events during the war, and it imposed them on a single family. The affluent Minivers have few troubles before the war begins, but events quickly accelerate. The son, Vin, joins the RAF as a pilot; the father, Clem, volunteers to assist in the Dunkirk evacuation; the family's home is bombed and they spend their nights in a bomb shelter on their property; the mother, Kay, disarms a wounded German pilot after being subject to his war rhetoric about German world domination; and the wounded begin appearing in town and at church services. However, life goes on, and Vin marries their wealthy neighbor Carol Beldon. A rose, named Mrs. Miniver, wins the local village competition after a generous impulse from the ruling aristocrat—Carol's grandmother—who abdicates her yearly win in favor of an ordinary gardener. Carol delivers a speech about how she knows she may only have Vin for a brief time, but in a raid, ironically Carol instead is killed, which devastates the family. Vin rises to the occasion, mourning his young wife and brief marriage. In the film's final scene, the town is gathered for Carol's funeral. Vin moves from his family's pew to join Carol's grandmother and with her sings "Onward, Christian Soldiers" while RAF fighters on the attack can be glimpsed through a gaping hole in the church's roof. The town stands together in grief and solidarity, a microcosm of the British nation. The film won six Academy Awards, including Best Picture, and its title became a catch phrase, as in this story H.D. recounts to Bryher: "I was stopped on a lonely road by a terrific dispatch-rider, who drew up and asked me where Seal was. I think I was clever, as I told him the way to the post-office and said they could direct him better than I, thus killing two birds with one stone, because IF bogus, the P.O. would deal, and if O.K., I at least put him on the way to direction. All too, too, too Mrs. Miniver here!"[145]

Some Londoners were reduced to spending their summer holidays fishing from the banks of Hyde Park's Serpentine in orderly rows—part of the government's "holidays at home" program—but H.D. did on occasion take trips to the countryside. Eventually, travel became so difficult—one could only take what could be carried, which had to include towels, soap, cleaning supplies, and dry groceries for the entire trip—that she limited her excursions.[146] Bryher still managed the journey to visit Trenoweth in St. Keverne, Cornwall, a farm run by Bryher's childhood friend Doris Banfield and her husband. Bryher had written to H.D. in May 1940 that Trenoweth could provide a haven for them: "Now don't forget that I bought farm shares partly that Pup and yourself could go to Cornwall if a war occurred, over five years ago, so go there if things look nasty. Nowhere near London will be safe at all."[147] For a single summer excursion, however, H.D. more often chose the nearby Woodhall, Silvia Dobson's farm that was only twenty-nine miles from London. Situated between London and Dover, Woodhall was also located in "bomb alley," and Dobson was "in an aerial battle zone, in danger from jettisoned bombs, spent bullets, downed planes, dead or wounded airmen, dangling from parachutes as they jerked erratically to earth."[148] Had Britain been invaded, the passageway would have been directly through Woodhall.

Ecstatically glad to see H.D., Dobson documents their time in her memoirs, being careful to point out the many mistakes she sees in Barbara Guest's biography of H.D. For example, Guest claims that H.D. rode to London on a cart pulled by a donkey. Dobson retorts, "Actually Matilda, the donkey lived in Cornwall at Trenoweth. I asked Barbara to change this silly passage, but someone in the publisher's with a bizarre sense of humour left it in. H.D. enjoyed the three mile journey back and forth between Ightham Mote and Woodhall on the hay cart, but we could never take her up to London, as the car was chock-a-block with sacks of vegetables, eggs, salad greens, flowers, mushrooms, baskets of fruit. I was only able to drive her down once or perhaps twice."[149] In her letters to Bryher, H.D. describes her visits during August of 1942, 1943, and 1944, helping bring in the harvest and enjoying the countryside. In 1942 she wrote, "I picked 300 apples to the sound of channel-boomings. I wonder if you heard the gun-fire your end, hardly I think. But we are so near; Dover, Folkstone are so familiar, and I am glad to be here, out of town. I hope you are pleased at this foretaste of action, at long last. The girls who took the veg. on the local round said there was much scurrying of troops along one sector of the line. It's good I got here when I did, and I am glad I am not due up this week. . . . I expect this week and week-end will be very exciting." In 1944, bomb alley lived up to its name, and a Nazi flier bailed out of his plane and "was up a *very* tall tree all night. They had to rescue him by means of a tall ladder. They gave him a cup of tea, as per usual, & he gulped it down & then went sound asleep in his chair. Now he has gone from our lives!"[150] In general, H.D. reported to friends that she enjoyed her bucolic visits, except in 1942 when Dobson temporarily misplaced H.D.'s invaluable ration book.

Dobson and Woodhall emerged from the war largely unscathed:

> During 1944 the Nazi bombers, no longer confident about attacking Britain on moon-bright nights or during the day, sneaked in on the darkest of dark moonless nights. We called this "the darks." Also many planes, unwilling to face London's crack anti-aircraft teams, unloaded their freight of bombs in Kent or Surrey and hurried home. One hundred and forty-three bombs and land mines fell on or near our rural village. We had three near-misses, one so close that I got outside before the debris had settled back to earth, leaving a gigantic hole in the road outside Woodhall. Similar blasts had flattened houses. Our old Elizabethan cottage, built directly onto heavy clay soil without foundations, swayed, shook off dust, yet remained intact. Twice during the war we had to evacuate while bomb squads disposed of unexploded bombs, embedded in our field. The heavy clay soil, so difficult to work, saved us from a great deal of damage. In the holes left we buried tin cans and bottles.[151]

From 1940 until 1944, Dobson tolerated these bombing raids because she had chosen to be part of an essential war activity—she was helping feed the English people and had joined the Women's Land Army.

"National Service Women's Land Army," ©Imperial War Museums (PST 5996).

Reap the Harvest of Victory

In very public ways, women's labor played a crucial role in World War II. Some women, like Perdita, drove mobile canteens and ambulances; other women were fire watchers; and still others grew food for the nation as part of the Women's Land Army, an army that fought its battles in the fields. Accustomed to importing its food from throughout the empire, Britain realized it needed to produce more of its food at home, as in World War I. In June 1939, even before war was officially declared, Britain created the Women's Land Army, which was headed by philanthropist Lady Denman, described by Vita Sack-ville-West as "the most competent and experienced of chairmen," who fought an uphill battle championing the value of women's labor.[152] The Land Girls, as they were called, were volunteers at the beginning, at least a third coming from London and the northern cities, and most had no farm experience. They were expected to work in excess of fifty-hour weeks at wages less than male agricultural workers and less than women serving in the forces. More than 80,000 women served as Land Girls, producing 70 percent of Britain's food by 1943.[153] Stodgy farmers and farming unions finally recognized the significance of women working on the land: farms continued to produce even with many men gone to fight, and Hitler was unable to starve Britain out. Once peace was declared, the Land Girls were not released, however, and the Women's Land Army continued its work until October 1950, when five hundred Land Girls paraded past Buckingham Palace to commemorate the disbandment of their army. Unlike their male counterparts involved in the war effort, these women were not welcomed back into the general workforce, nor did the nation help them find suitable jobs. Only in 2008 were these women even eligible to apply for an official badge celebrating their contributions to the war effort.

Dobson struggled to find a way to contribute to the war effort.[154] First, she signed up as an escort for children being evacuated through the Children's Overseas Reception Board (CORB), a British governmental organization moving children out of England and into Canada, Australia, New Zealand, South Africa, and the United States between July and September 1940. This effort came to an abrupt halt in September when German U-boats torpedoed and sank the SS *City of Benares*, which was evacuating children to Canada. H.D. wrote to a cousin in the United States that she was "greatly shocked by the loss of those children—it is incredible. A friend was to sail on that boat, and at the last moment, providentially was prevented. She was taking a child across, now the mother is deeply grateful that the little boy was prevented going at the last."[155] This friend was Dobson, who wrote in her memoir, "Before I was called up, ships with children being evacuated were sunk and the scheme stopped."[156] Dobson instead found work with children evacuated to Britain but needed something more permanent to prevent the government from assigning her a job: "What to do? What war work should I attempt before some Ministry claimed me as clerk, bottle-washer, office stooge? . . . Why not grow food? Hitler meant to starve us out. Growing vegetables, rearing hens for eggs, collecting surplus produce to sell in London might be a valid way to combat Nazism. I decided to join the Land Army, was accepted, given a uniform, and told to report to Swanley Agricultural College for a crash course lasting six weeks."[157] Lord Haw-Haw, the name given to the English-language broadcast by Nazi Germany to Britain from 1939 to 1945, taunted the British with threats of starvation.[158] For an isolated island, the threat was real, and women like Dobson stepped forward to meet the challenge of feeding the nation.

Dobson and her siblings were already renting a farmhouse with more than two acres of land in Woodhall. With the possibilities those acres offered in mind, Dobson biked the twenty miles from Woodhall to Swanley Horticultural College, Kent, a top agricultural school. With other volunteers—secretaries, dancers, college students, factory workers, store clerks—she joined the graduating class there to learn how to farm. About her experiences at Swanley, Dobson wrote,

> Joining a hundred potential Land Army recruits sobered me. Here were dedicated forward-looking young women. I enjoyed more the four-year students, taking degree courses, who helped us with practical work, hoeing, weeding, digging, pruning, harvesting ripe crops, learning to plough. One serious agriculturist, leading us to dig up turnips, gave a slender ballet-dancer the huge wheel barrow to push to the site. When she put it down, he called us all to watch, then said, "Turn the barrow round, so that it faces the way you have to go when it's full to over-flowing. Heavy work is no picnic. Learn to save yourselves trouble by thinking ahead."[159]

Farm equipment was built to be used by men, not slender ballerinas, and the women had to learn how to manage equipment never intended for someone of their size or strength, as well as develop necessary skills: "hoeing, weeding, picking and storing fruit, learning to plough, trench ground, prune, graft, sow seed."[160] At the end of her course, Dobson was disappointed to find that she was expected to work for a farmer or landowner rather than on her own. The official line was that a two-month course might have given her enough knowledge to work for someone else but not enough to succeed independently as a business owner. Undaunted, Dobson returned the uniform but was allowed to keep the Certificate of Competence. She was ready to farm.[161]

Back at Woodhall, Dobson began her business, a state-sanctioned escape from gender roles; she donned pants and "bought a cultivator, seed, plants, extra tools; dug up the huge back field. The rows of vegetables I raised and tended." She needed cash to purchase more seed, fertilizer, and supplies, as well as to pay the neighbor's daughter Dorothy, her sisters, and friends who worked in her business at different times. To fund this enterprise, Dobson asked her friends in London if she might bring up a weekly bundle consisting of produce, eggs, and flowers. Eggs, a scarce and important source of protein, were in short supply, and so Dobson determined to raise chickens herself: "The growers who provided me with mushrooms told me of an Edenbridge expert, commissioned by the Ministry of Food to find a breed which produced table birds for rapidly expanding cruise liner tables, had marans to sell. As cruise travel no longer functioned, breeding stock was going cheap. My pullets laid delightful dark brown eggs." For flowers, she gathered what she could find: "I roamed through bluebell woods, picked primroses from mossy banks, found foxgloves in our secret wood. . . . Friends grew extra produce in their gardens for beleaguered Londoners. I rejuvenated our over-grown apple, plum and cherry trees, by making blossom bunches."[162]

Dobson's London friends enthusiastically endorsed her plan, and her customer base began to grow from personal friends like H.D., whom she supplied every week throughout the war, to at least seventy households, ranging from the head of the London Fire Brigade to the butler of Lord Crookshanks, chancellor of England (with whom she took sherry on occasion), to the canteen at St. George's Hospital. Dobson wrote, "We really enjoyed our small customers, single people, newly-weds, wives with husbands in the services. Once our wholesaler had a crate of bananas, the first we had seen since pre-war days. We were able to sell a couple to anyone who wanted them, and have some for ourselves." Ponies were evacuated to Woodhall and were used for local transportation, but the petrol rations allowed the trips to London. A twice-a-week routine developed: the car was packed with produce on Mondays; Dobson and a friend left for town early on Tuesday to make deliveries; and they returned home late in the day, after lunch at Harrods.[163] In early 1944, however, the gas ration was cut such that only one trip per week was possible, and by May, when gasoline became further rationed, Dobson was no longer able to take produce to London. She started sending her bundles by rail, but the lack of reliable transportation spelled the end of her farming at Woodhall. The produce she had provided sustained H.D. and Bryher, and it is in 1944 that H.D.'s troubles with a dire lack of food begin in earnest.

"Dig for Victory Now," ©Imperial War Museums (PST 17009).

The Kitchen Is the Key to Victory

In Britain, rationing began in January 1940; it was the government's effort to equitably spread the limited resources to all people, rich and poor, and despite its many shortfalls, it prevented starvation. Before the war began, Britain, as a colonial power, imported 60 percent of its food supplies, and because Britain is an island, those supplies had to arrive by sea. Once Germany set its sights on conquering Britain, it patrolled the waters, bombing ships carrying munitions and food, causing shortages. On September 29, 1939, soon after Britain declared war on Germany, households in Britain filled out a form listing all of the people who lived in each home, and everyone was issued an identity card, which had to be carried at all times, and a ration book, marked with one's individual number. Exotic foods like bananas disappeared from store shelves immediately, but even British staples became increasingly hard to find. Nineteen forty began with the rationing of sugar (sweets largely disappeared from store shelves, and icing was banned), butter, bacon, and ham—foods that provided the crucial fat for cooking. In February, paper was rationed; in March, meat appeared on the ration list. Tea, margarine, and cooking fats followed soon after. Although amounts were adjusted through the war, a typical weekly adult ration looked like this:

Butter	2 oz
Bacon and ham	4 oz
Margarine	4 oz
Sugar	8–12 oz
Tea	2 oz
Cheese	2 oz
Milk	3 pints
Eggs	1 fresh egg, then 1 dried egg packet every four weeks
Jam	8 oz
Meat	Up to the value of 1 shilling, 2 pence [approximately $3–4 in 2013]

By 1941, jam, marmalade, syrup, cheese, and coal were rationed, and the distribution of eggs and milk was controlled. In 1942, rice, dried fruit, soap, tinned tomatoes and peas, all domestic fuels, and biscuits made the ration list. At the war's end, food became even scarcer as people poured back into London and other parts of Britain, where food supplies were still severely limited. It wasn't until 1946 that bread was rationed, although for years before that it was often inedible, and in 1947 the British staple potatoes were rationed. Finally, in 1948, food supplies began to recover. Bread, flour, potato, and jam rationing ended; and in 1950, many of the foods craved by the populace came off the rationing scheme: canned and dried fruit, chocolate biscuits, syrup, jelly, gasoline, soap, and tea. By 1953, sweets, eggs, cream, and sugar became widely available, but it was not until 1954 that rationing ended, with freely available butter, cheese, cooking fats, and, most important, meat. Throughout the war, protein had been largely missing from the general diet, and that lack, which lasted for some people for fourteen years, irrevocably affected the populace's health and lifespan.

H.D. and Bryher put up a brave front for outsiders, consistently maintaining that they were eating well, but between themselves, they admitted the truth. Bryher wrote H.D. as early as 1941 that "it is getting awfully difficult now about food. . . . Miss Voules, I think it was, said rook pie is excellent but not to use the legs, only the breasts."[164] As the war progressed, the deprivations intensified, and rationing had serious long-term effects. In the spring of 1946, H.D. was taken ill, an illness that belongs to the postwar period but one rooted in the war privations and trauma. Literary critics have made much of this 1946 illness, some even designating it a serious nervous breakdown, a nonmedical term too often applied to women. Definitively diagnosing H.D. at this late date is nigh impossible, but limited information about her illness is obtainable in correspondence. However, reliable details remain sketchy and assembling the available evidence a sometimes elusive interpretive exercise.

In January 1946, H.D. was finalizing plans to lecture at Bryn Mawr for a semester, an opportunity facilitated by Pearson, who recognized the difficulties of living in London. He longed to have H.D. in the States, and he hoped the trip would offer her time in which to properly recover from the exigencies of war.[165] However, by February H.D. was ill and this trip canceled at the last minute, even as Perdita hopefully waited for her mother's arrival. H.D. and Pearson meant to reschedule, and Bryn Mawr officials extended an open offer for her visit, but she never did deliver the planned lectures. It seems that H.D. became depressed and suffered from hallucinations, delusions, and memory loss.[166] In her letters to Bryher, Perdita repeatedly offered to return to London to help, and in March, she commented that she was "most impressed by the way you've rallied the experts around you" to help H.D. and that plans to move H.D. to Switzerland were under way: "Is our Kat [H.D.] still flying out in great style, with the blessings of the Red Cross. I'm longing to hear of developments." By April, however, Perdita wrote, "I'm disturbed by the developments about Kat. How naughty of her to refuse to move. Obviously, London is the last place for her to stick in."[167] Many of the letters among Perdita, Bryher, H.D., and their friends offer limited information about H.D.'s illness or even dissemble, so as not to upset, which amplifies the problem of discovering the true nature of H.D.'s illness and treatment. However, Bryher repeatedly informs friends that H.D. is ill from meningitis and malnutrition, as in her letter to Jordan: "The doctor here found her suffering from the effects of meningitis, prolonged malnutrition and nerve shock from the war."[168] According to Bryher, during the war H.D. lost forty pounds from her svelte frame, and H.D. self-consciously comments in letters that she has lost a number of teeth.[169]

On May 13, 1946, H.D. traveled to Seehof, Privat Klinik Brunner in Küsnacht on Lake Zurich, a private hospital run by Dr. Theodore Brunner. The hospitals in Britain were still overwhelmed by the war and had few resources upon which to draw. In contrast, in Switzerland, where Bryher and H.D. had a home, rations were a third higher, and many foods were not rationed; additionally, as a hospital patient, H.D. was accorded extras in important protein sources like milk and eggs. According to Bryher, "The Swiss doctor says it is partly complete exhaustion due to war shock and bad food and conditions and so for six weeks she is not to write letters nor read but is to lie in their beautiful garden and eat and sleep. Then he is sure that she will completely recover."[170] Switzerland had largely escaped the bombing inflicted upon London, and the scenery lacked the physical marks of war: "Coming to Switzerland is like stepping into paradise from hell. The quality of the food and of everything is superb, there is sun, and everything is unscarred," Bryher wrote to Wolle.[171] Perdita was pleased with the news she received from H.D. and commented to Bryher that H.D. "sounds happy in her select establishment, quite her Kat self once more; I like the idea of her pottering around in those gardens—what could be more suitable."[172]

However, H.D.'s letters in September belie Perdita's optimistic opinion. It is unclear whether a new crisis struck in September, whether the Klinik had been misinforming Bryher and others about H.D.'s progress, or whether H.D.'s anger over being stymied in her wish to leave reached a breaking point. On September 26, 1946, H.D., in a disturbing letter, wrote Pearson that she was trying to leave the Klinik and that she felt letters and parcels were not being delivered to her nor letters she wrote being mailed. She too offered the information that she suffered from cerebral meningitis, but she wrote that she did not understand why she had been hospitalized:

> I was here for 5 months, enduring *shock treatment* of a most pernicious nature. My papers were taken away, I was locked up without food or water & injected with _____ [*sic*] I don't know what. Today, for the first time in 7 months, I saw Bryher with Walter Schmideberg. She seemed well & happy. I don't understand it at all. The flight alone, after 2 months in bed, was enough to kill one. It was my first day up, & after a long motor-run, I was bundled into a curious plane by a doctor whom I scarcely knew. It took us 10 hours to get here, instead of the usual 2. Fletcher wrote me. I answered, please tell him. Evidently, my letters were never sent out. I wrote Susan & yourself & Perdita, all the time. Could you send P. a wire & say I am all right, that I hope to get to London, then USA, *to see her*. I am sure Bryher meant it all for the best. Please do not disillusion her.[173]

It appears that Bryher had been with H.D. in her early days at Klinik Brunner, but her presence and letters upset H.D., so she was asked to stay away, as were H.D.'s friends. Bryher's letters offer H.D. calm support and the assurance that they will be together as soon as H.D. is well, which will come through eating, gaining weight, and sleeping.

In a letter dated September 29, 1946, and addressed to "my darling Hilda," worth quoting in its entirety, Bryher explains the situation:

> You want to know what has happened and why you are at Küsnacht. Last February you were taken very ill and for a time I think you did not know any of us. It was then that Dr. Carroll—who is Irish—came to take charge. He wanted to send you to a sanatorium in England but the food and heating conditions had got so much worse that the Bear [Walter Schmideberg] and I thought the only thing to do was to try to get you to Switzerland.
>
> The Bear and I came ahead to find a place for you. We consulted with a great friend of Professor Freud in Basel and we found See Hof [*sic*] through him. I saw some other places but you would not have been happy in them, for they were like hospitals. We arranged with great difficulty to have you flown out to Zurich. We could not get a whole

plane so had to agree to share with a lady who was coming out with her children.

You flew first to Paris, there they had to land to re-fuel and then on to Zurich. Dr. Carroll brought you out with one of the nurses. They returned to England two days later.

There are no enemy countries now. And no upheavals.

All your friends have been told that you had meningitis and that you are recovering—as indeed you are—in Switzerland, as you had had to be in the mountains after the last war. All your letters have reached their destination except for two you sent to Sir Humphrey Milford who is no longer with the Oxford Press and whose address I cannot find. The Oxford Press reply always that letters should be sent to them, Sir Humphrey having retired.

Everybody—including Perdita—knows that you have been under a terrible strain during the war and all are waiting for you to be quite well again.

You have to make up a lot of weight that you have lost, sleep much better, and listen to all that Dr. Brunner tells you—then very soon he will allow me to come and fetch you wherever you would like to go. But until you are recovered no doctor anywhere would let you leave the sanatorium for you might become very ill without proper care.

Philip is looking after all your financial affairs, everything is being paid by him for you, the flat and all its contents are being cared for, your papers are locked up, as are your books, till the moment comes when you need them.

I beg of you only to listen to the wise counsel of Dr. Brunner, eat well and sleep well, then we shall be re-united the sooner. It is no question of sanity or otherwise, it is just that you, like hundreds of other English people, have suffered a terrible strain through the war and lost temporarily your memory. Switzerland is full of people being helped to be well.[174]

Still, H.D. sought to leave the clinic, trying to enlist Bryher's help as well as writing to the British Consulate for assistance, but she did not have the means to leave since she was there on medical orders and had no access to her money (movement and use of currencies were strictly regulated in the war and postwar years).

Although H.D. felt betrayed, as expressed in her accusatory and, in turn, apologetic letters to Bryher during this brief period, Bryher repeatedly promised that as soon as she was well, they would be together, H.D. could live where she liked, and H.D.'s friends were waiting upon her recovery. Furthermore, she sent assurances that H.D.'s things were in storage for her, that their incomes were protected, and that her flat at Lowndes Square had been let to a friend but only because unoccupied housing, during the shortage, could be seized by the government. In the next few weeks, H.D.'s recovery accelerated, and by mid-October she and Bryher were planning for her release. Bryher repeatedly encouraged H.D. to remain in Switzerland because living conditions had deteriorated so in London, and when Bryher joined her, she brought all the books, papers, and such H.D. had requested. In letters, H.D. consequently apologized to her family, writing to Pearson that "I am grieved and sorry that I was such a trouble to everyone. Will you thank all who helped, with goodness & self-sacrifice. . . . I have been very ill indeed." She lamented missing her visit to Bryn Mawr and ironically wrote about her preparations that "I got so excited—I expect I overdid things, as usual. Well, it earned me this holiday, at any rate. In a month's time, I expect to be at: Alexandria Hotel, Lausanne."[175]

On November 21, H.D. moved to the Alexandria Hotel in Lausanne, a fortuitous choice since the harsh 1946–47 winter further brutalized battered Londoners. The intense cold spells and uncommon accumulations of snow stifled transportation, fuel for heating and cooking was further limited, industrial production dropped, the pound lost a third of its value, the Cold War began, and hunger increased as crops and farm animals were lost. Morale plummeted after the initial euphoria at the end of the war, and Herring wrote in his March 1946 editorial for *Life and Letters Today* that "no one will deny that the general feeling is we are losing the peace nicely," in large part through the continuing shortages: "the Prime Minister promises a lessening of austerity. But he does it by promising 'Half-way Back to Pre-War Standards this Year.' The first two words are a mistake; 'half-way' still implies division, reduction rather than multiplication and increase, and 'back' is not a looking-forward word."[176] Bryher was forced to close Kenwin for the winter because fuel was also short in Switzerland, and she spent that winter, and many more, with Elsie Volkart in Vaud. Only a few minutes from H.D. on the bus, Bryher told friends that they met almost every day to shop or share a meal. The food supplies remain a constant topic in letters; H.D. was steadily gaining weight with the better supplies Switzerland had to offer, and by December 1946 she had regained eight pounds.

H.D. may have suffered from meningitis—a bacterial or viral infection of the membranes covering the brain and spinal cord—whose symptoms can include fever, nausea, severe headache, stiff neck, sensitivity to light, seizures, sleepiness, weight loss, and, significantly, changes in one's mental status. It is the wording of Bryher's letter, quoted earlier, that "your friends *have been told* that you had meningitis" [emphasis added] that suggests dissemblance. H.D. may have been suffering from a different infectious disease like tuberculosis, although the telling TB cough is not mentioned in letters. Other less dire possibilities include a myriad of vitamin deficiencies like scurvy, which is caused by a lack of vitamin C and can cause tooth loss, tiredness, pain in the legs and joints, shortness of breath, and easily bruised skin; pellagra, caused by a lack of niacin with symptoms of mental confusion, aggression, dermatitis, insomnia, and general weakness; or even anemia, which can be caused by iron and vitamin deficiencies. Whatever the contemporary diagnosis might be, Bryher's consistent explanation of H.D.'s illness as a result of shock (what might currently be termed post-traumatic stress disorder), malnutrition, and weight loss ring true, thus highlighting the role of food in H.D.'s life during World War II.

For H.D., Bryher, and even Perdita, food remained a preoccupation for the rest of their lives. Even once rationing was over and food was plentiful, they often remarked on the availability and quality of food in their letters. Once having experienced malnutrition, they were constantly aware of food and thankful for it—a lifelong mental and physical preoccupation directly caused by war shortages and rationing. In her memoir *The Days of Mars*, Bryher commented that "the rationing system in England was absurd. 'Bread is unrationed,' the bureaucrats said proudly but it was not even sawdust; we wondered what it could contain and we knew it was unrationed because it was uneatable. It turned a particularly livid hue of green within a few hours and was so hard that the populace referred to it as 'our secret weapon.'"[177] In 1943, when H.D. and Bryher became ill with the common "blitz-flu," Jordan suggested that vitamin C and fruit would be healing. H.D. was amused: "We laughed ourselves almost sick over your good suggestion of lemons when we had colds—as my dear, this country has not SEEN a lemon for years—literally!"[178] Bryher assured Jordan that they had a doctor providing vitamins, and she clarified the shortage of natural vitamin C:

We can still get aspirin but such a thing as a lemon hasn't been seen here for nearly three years. A few oranges arrive occasionally but are kept for children under five or sent to hospitals. A doctor friend gave us a very small quantity of medical lemon juice, such as they used to use on ships, nearly three years ago and we keep this for emergencies. Actually we were both lucky last summer as we were with friends in the country who grew some soft fruit but lots of townspeople have scarcely seen fruit since 1940 except for a few apples or plums. Sometimes canned fruit is released on "points" but as each person only gets twenty points a month, and they are usually priced at twelve or sixteen points, it is not a very good buy as you spend all your month's ration on one tin. We have to give points for rice, tapioca, crackers, tinned meat, tinned fish, breakfast cereals, syrup, our equivalent of your molasses, and lots of other things. You have to be awfully careful as once you have given your points up, there are no more till the next month.[179]

The points system allowed consumers choices between food options, but, as Bryher explained, those choices had to be carefully considered. The price of items in points—and one had to have money as well as points because the points permitted the purchase but did not pay for it—varied among items and over time, depending on scarcity and demand. Bryher once explained how she had spent her weekly twenty points: "I got a tin of syrup for eight points, a half pound of dates for eight points, and a half pound of biscuits for four points. Meat is too costly in points." Duly shocked, Jordan responded by sending food and seeds, so that they could provide themselves with some staples—seed was as hard to come by as the produce grown from it. Bryher thanked her for the seed: "It is so amusing, you know we have allotments everywhere, in the parks, square gardens etc, the seeds have been carried by the wind all over the place and I found some cress growing out of the pavement in a quiet street the other day. It was most odd."[180]

Restaurants were still an option if British citizens could afford them, but luxuries were frowned upon as being unpatriotic. The restaurants' offerings were limited by what they could find to cook and what they could charge; the government capped prices so that the rich ate more like regular people and prohibited serving both meat and fish in one meal. The government itself began running restaurants offering a filling meal, particularly useful to the many people involved in war work. H.D. and Bryher ate lunch out as often as possible, which required money but not points, and their household roles were clearly delineated: H.D. cooked and Bryher shopped. H.D., never an accomplished cook, clarified that her style of cooking was uncomplicated: "though I do not do very much hard work, I am the one who beats up the egg or rather mixes the egg-powder and makes the custard and sometimes does a bit of freezing in the [refrigerator], which fortunately is in good working order and of course, coffee and tea."[181] Bryher explained to Jordan that H.D. "does the cooking too, breakfast and dinner in the evening and tea . . . I do the shopping . . . a very long and tedious job and one has to carry back most of the food."[182] Transportation was increasingly scarce, so valuable calories were expended simply in locating food and carrying it home. Along with the shopping, Bryher dealt with the ration books. When she was out of town, she sent H.D. detailed instructions about what to do, and she carefully considered which grocers to use because one had to register with a specific grocery store: "I remembered a bit of advice from the First World War. Never register all the members of a household at the same shop. One part of Lowndes Square was in Westminster but our side was in Chelsea so as soon as I got my ration book I took it not to Hilda's grocer but to a large neighboring store."[183] Every time new ration books were issued, Bryher had to queue, sometimes for hours, simply to retrieve theirs, and it was crucially important not to lose them. When they were given luxuries, H.D. and Bryher treated them differently; Bryher liked to save them, and H.D. wanted to enjoy them, an insight H.D. shared with Jordan: Bryher "is a bit of a squirrel and likes to feel the things she likes BEST are there for the future, I think it better to eat the best while we can . . . so there we are Spratt and Mrs. J. S. complete."[184]

The new dearth of imported food led to slogans like "dig for victory" and a governmental push for citizens to grow their own food. Rose bushes were replaced by cabbages in tiny front gardens, on estate gardens like Renishaw's, and around government buildings. However, while the vegetables might be filling, they did not solve the dire need for protein. Some Londoners had begun addressing the need for protein themselves, keeping rabbits, chickens, and even goats in the city. (Valuable commodities like rabbits were taken along on even brief holidays to safeguard them from poaching neighbors.) In a move as uncharacteristic as becoming the family's cook, H.D., along with Bryher, began raising chickens. During the spring of 1942, Bryher kept Jordan updated about the state of their flock: "My pet amusement is collecting scraps in a bag for our chickens. I think it is a feat to keep chickens in mid London. Actually a friend has them and looks after them in a little yard. It was my job to get them through farmer friends, it was very hard to buy any last autumn, and to collect food. They have a ration card!"[185] Domestic animals were closely regulated by the government to ensure that even this food was equally shared, and people were expected to feed their animals with scraps. Bryher wrote about their chicken scheme that "we share the eggs. They have been the greatest asset these last months, worth literally their weight in gold. We are not allowed to keep more than 12 and have, actually, 11. We can keep more but if we do, have to surrender the eggs. Most people keep about eight. My very pompous lawyer has given up his lawn to be a chicken run. . . . he lives about half an hour out and somebody else I know has six." Some barnyard trouble was solved in April: "One of our hens started eating the eggs! This was too much after all our scrap hunts for their food so she was killed promptly. I think it is because the run is so small but after all central London was not exactly intended for poultry farming, was it? People a bit further out with real gardens are all going in for goats."[186] Their troublesome chicken proved to be a delicious dinner herself. As with chickens, groups of friends banded together to raise pigs—the popular pig clubs—which were controlled by byzantine governmental regulations. Herring felt cheated when the government seized half of his slaughtered pig, the option being to relinquish an inordinate amount of coupons. He worried the logistics involved discouraged people from raising livestock, when quite the opposite was desired.[187]

Bryher often commented that the Swiss had prepared admirably for the war and stockpiled foodstuffs early, focusing on quality rather than quantity. She wrote about Britain that "our food has been the worst planned of anything we've done during the war, I think."[188] In her memoirs, she reinforced this opinion: "It was said in England that we gave the children in England an adequate diet but that was propaganda. The ones I met were always hungry and their parents undernourished. Of course this is not the picture that was presented to the world."[189] Bryher was particularly fond of *The Red Tapeworm*—she even became friends with its author, Compton Mackenzie and his wife, Faith—a popular book that criticized government waste and bureaucracy, and she saved newspaper clippings offering similar criticisms. These clippings memorialize governmental waste of paper for job applications when citizens were being exhorted to use paper sparingly; the loss of 300 dozen eggs because the Eggs Branch did not properly market and disperse them; the prohibition against families making syrup with which to make jam because sugar was excisable; and the ridiculous regulations involved in keeping a pig because government officials did not understand the farmers' lingo. Articles excoriate on one hand the lack of employment for skilled people as an example of the mishandling of labor, with factories claiming to need workers and then laying them off, and on the other, the wasteful manufacture of tens of thousands of shells destined for the scrap heap. An August 4, 1941, clipping describes "the machine" as the governmental mechanizations into which applications for anything are placed and which, after a very lengthy wait, spew forth nonsense: "I have decided that I know the Machine's name. It is not Demogorgon. It is Civil Service Procedure—and it is the same Machine that addles everything, from eggs to aircraft production, delighting in forms and delaying contracts. Some day—unless Parliament (which it undoubtedly fears) intervenes—it might even lose us the war." Bryher even collected wickedly hilarious cartoons, including one from July 14, 1942, with the tag line,

Mr. Mullins: Neither of these lads looks dangerous—just stupid.
Inspector Vanstone: They both work at the Ministry of Information.

A similar clipping from 1944 reads, "It is a pity that the House does not hear more from Mr. Stuart. He made a neat speech at the Press Gallery luncheon to Mr. Eden, and in the course of it quoted a motto which someone had suggested for the Ministry of Information. It was: 'Give us the straw and we will drop the bricks.'"[190]

Clothing was also rationed, and coupon books were issued, which basically allowed an adult one new outfit per year. Moreover, the design of clothing was controlled so that material stretched farther. The iconic photos of thin women in tight skirts were a direct product of scarcity: little excess food to encourage overeating paired with a skirt width, collar size, and suit cut thinned to use less material. Along with clothing, soap was rationed. Bryher wrote to a friend, "It is all right if one can send things to a laundry and if there are no children, but a big problem for a large family."[191] Civilians were exhorted to "mend and make do," and they did. H.D. mentioned in a 1942 letter that she has taken in three pairs of shoes to be patched;[192] by 1943 Bryher says that despite the dirt in London, "most people have given up stockings";[193] Bryher collected free camel hair from the zoo to be spun into warm cloth (her resultant coat was warm but never lost its gamey smell);[194] and in 1944 they were loath to take down blackout curtains because to replace them would require dress coupons.[195] A raincoat cost Bryher twelve of her precious coupons.[196] Despite their financial assets, Bryher and H.D. avoided the black market; nonetheless, they did on occasion evade clothing coupons, once for the sake of summer sandals.[197] Clothes rationing led to unusual outfits. Bryher wrote, "I met a lady a few days ago, she must have been seventy and she had on a little fur coat coming midway between her waist and her knees, riding breeches, old fashioned buttoned leggings and a neat little bonnet on her white hair. Yet nobody even looked at her though I must confess I laughed all day whenever I thought of it."[198] H.D. once enthusiastically thanked Jordan for her gift of "pants" (underwear in British English): "the 'pants' arrived o.k., and are a joy to behold. Did you know there were SEVEN pairs?"[199]

Furniture, particularly anything practical, was in short supply. While purchasing furniture in wartime seems a luxury, flats were bombed, families begun, and homeless relatives moved in, sometimes making furniture a necessity. The Utility Furniture Scheme was created in 1942 and lasted until 1952. With little timber available, this furniture was designed to be strong and efficient, which resulted in starkly simplistic designs that resemble Shaker furniture, not a popular style at the time, and of wildly variable quality. For Christmas in 1942, Bryher gave friends rare practical items and was quite overcome with H.D.'s gift: "I gave as Christmas presents this year shopping baskets filled with scrubbing and boot brushes, household remedies, herb teas and toilet paper. They were an immense success. But Hilda—how we shall never know—secured for me that long since vanished triumph, a kitchen chair. You see, if you wanted a stuffed kangaroo or a jeweled table you would probably find same easily, it is the everyday things that are with the dinosaurs, extinct."[200] Furthermore, paint was a rare commodity: "Of course here you can't get any paint at all, unless your place has been blitzed and you fill up innumerable forms or unless you can prove the outside is falling to pieces. Then you get only a standard utility paint in a range of about three colors. I can't think why they had to choose such ugly ones. We were allowed to have the office distempered as it had just been repaired from the blitz but all the paint we could get was a most horrible chocolate color. More than austere." Another commodity in short supply was privacy; since packages were no longer wrapped in shops, even meager purchases were open to public inspection: "yesterday I met our neighbor coming in and she was dangling a scrubbing brush and I had a lamp I'd taken to be repaired!

We stood and laughed at each other. The funniest is somebody carrying a toothbrush. I also saw yesterday and was most amused, a very prim white haired old lady in her husband's tweed pants and a tin hat. I expect she had been fire watching."[201]

American friends and family began sending packages of food and necessities, for which H.D. and Bryher were constantly thanking them. Jordan sent valuable chocolate and cigarettes, which brought the police to H.D.'s door since they were not allowed, as she repeatedly explained to Jordan, and Baker sent food, stockings, toothpaste, sweets, soap, tinsel, tea, scarves, candles, lipsticks in a variety of reds, and bobby pins, which delighted Perdita, H.D. assured her: "Perdita came in last night for her leave—she was not here for Christmas—and screamed, she simply howled with joy over the bob-pins, she has been in despair. However, I only gave her one of the sheets, will be very prim and proper myself, for once."[202] When Pearson arrived in London, he had access to American service supplies, and he often brought them cigarettes, fruit, and once a rare pineapple. The cigarettes were smoked, the fruit eaten, but something as singular as a pineapple deserved a celebration: "We decided that the correct thing to do with such a pine apple of the Hesperides was to have a Valentine party of all the poets we could collect. This depends upon the health of the pineapple . . . tomorrow I take expert advice upon it. . . . We feel each poet should preserve a segment of pine-apple as a symbol of so great a moment."[203]

In 1944, a letter finally arrived from Sylvia Beach in Paris. H.D. wrote to her, "I can not tell you what your letter meant. We just let out a howl of joy and it is our one topic of conversation everywhere. . . . The thing is, the DOORS OUT OF HELL have opened a crack—O, when they swing back finally!"[204] Beginning immediately, Beach constantly wrote to H.D. and Bryher thanking them for packages of food and clothing. Knowing that they were still rationed themselves, Beach wrote, "But you are short of everything too, dear Bryher, and mustn't bleed yourselves from every vein for us."[205] Her thanks became a constant refrain in letters that underscored the depth and length of the privations. American friends like Moore and Sarton were recruited to send food to Beach, and she received CARE packages, just as H.D. and Bryher did. CARE was founded in 1945 for Americans wishing to help European friends, family, and even strangers survive after the war ended. Costing $10 each, parcels were guaranteed to arrive within four months. The first CARE packages held the following contents:

- 1 pound of beef in broth
- 1 pound of steak and kidneys
- 8 ounces of liver loaf
- 8 ounces of corned beef
- 12 ounces of luncheon loaf (like Spam®)
- 8 ounces of bacon
- 2 pounds of margarine
- 1 pound of lard
- 1 pound of fruit preserves
- 1 pound of honey
- 1 pound of raisins
- 1 pound of chocolate
- 2 pounds of sugar
- 8 ounces of egg powder
- 2 pounds of whole-milk powder
- 2 pounds of coffee[206]

Even in 1948 Beach commented, "Those people have calculated just what we need most—milk, butter, chocolate, coffee etc and the lovely white flour for making cakes, and the sugar—phew—and the bacon, even soap. We get almost no soap to this day, strange to say, and no milk yet, nor chocolate, and it's like in England for parts—sugar—it's meager."[207]

From her friends who longed to care for her after her ordeal, Beach requested and received coffee, cigarettes, cocoa, chocolate, lard, bacon, rice (which was a joke because rice was unavailable to anyone), six yards of muslin for chemises, tea towels, pillowcases, butter, cakes, marmalade, Nescafe, sugar, nylon stockings, olive oil, soap, roast beef, pork sausage, and sardines. She wrote Bryher that "all so welcome in the present famine—'une aubaine' [a godsend] Adrienne [Monnier] calls your parcels. I hope you get some things for yourself from the US—I know how short you are of food this winter—and Madame Wiel says you are very thin. The privations, I'm told, are worse than in any of the war years even. I am very sorry to hear that. As for us, I don't know what we would eat or wear if it were not for the Bryher parcels."[208] In 1949, finally, Beach assured Bryher that the CARE packages could be canceled because they had access to all the foodstuffs except coffee.

However, in 1942 and 1943, the war simply stretched on, and German air raids returned, as H.D. wrote Jordan: "it brings back the old, worst days and unsettles one's tummy. Some people got *sea-sick* in the worst days."[209] Four years of bombing had been a very long time, and the official word was that "one out of every five houses in England was damaged, in some way & *not* counting just broken windows!"[210] Bryher recounted a story about a friend whose children were "machine gunned the other day. They are six and nine and were just leaving school. Fortunately they were not hurt. But it is alarming for the mothers, even if the children, as in this case, regarded it as an adventure."[211] Plank caught tuberculosis from serving in the Home Guard—created by Anthony Eden and composed of the elderly and retired who still wanted to contribute to the war effort—most likely, Bryher believed, "as a result of racing round and getting wet." Bryher's mother-in-law passed away, and her father-in-law, then seventy-five years old, moved into their flat, making a small space smaller. "Pop" was eventually granted a compassionate visa to join his daughter in Long Island. The government was happy to rid itself of the responsibility for older people unable to contribute to the war effort; they were known as "useless mouths."[212] During blackouts, thieves began breaking into homes and stealing things; most people had little of value left, but everything is valuable in a time of extreme scarcity.[213] The government asked people to cut baths to once a week and to eliminate fires entirely; it prohibited photographs of people in public places, and it was almost impossible to get any photographs during the war; it even asked that people be sparing in their letters overseas, a request that particularly chafed. Throughout all the hardship, Bryher commented, H.D. continued to write: "I am amazed at Hilda—how she works, in spite of raids, austerity and general gloom."[214]

In 1943, Osbert Sitwell devised a plan to raise morale: a poetry reading. The event was called "A Reading by Famous Poets of Selections from Their Own Works," and it was held on April 14 in the Aeolian Hall on Bond Street. Already a star-studded event with the likes of the British Poet Laureate John Masefield, H.D., T. S. Eliot, Walter de la Mare, Vita Sackville-West, and Edith and Osbert Sitwell reading, it became one of *the* literary events of the war because the queen and the princesses Elizabeth and Margaret attended.[215] The event sold out quickly, and Bryher reported to Moore that "it would be much easier to say who was not in the audience than who was. They could have sold the hall out three times over and I was deluged with phone calls from people who thought I could get them tickets. I had taken mine as soon as it was announced. We knew, of course, what was likely to happen but naturally were not permitted to say."[216] Bryher went on to explain that the editor of the *Times Literary Supplement*, D. L. Murray, directed the event, and that the poets read in alphabetical order. During the intermission, the poets were presented to the queen and the princesses, a moment H.D. describes as "so very un-real and fairy-tale like to be curtseying . . . to Royalty."[217]

The program advertised the event as "In Aid of the French in Great Britain Fund." The Free French were troops committed to fighting against Germany after the fall of France in 1940. Led by General Charles de Gaulle, the Free French grew from merely the French troops in England and the remnants of the French navy to more than 300,000 regular troops by the time of the Normandy Invasion in June 1944. Equipped by the Americans, the Free French helped liberate France, and on August 26, 1944, de Gaulle triumphantly entered Paris. Herring, in the May 1943 issue of *Life and Letters Today*, characterized the poets who volunteered their time as "fighters—these whose wings are of Pegasus and who . . . were allowed to state their faith, one spring afternoon, at a reading to which the presence of Her Majesty the Queen gave the last graciousness of a May revel." Herring went on to describe H.D. as a poet who "evoked spontaneous applause by her grave conviction, both of matter and of manner."[218]

To Moore, Bryher wrote, "Well, what about our Hilda now? I do wish your Mother and yourself could have been with me last Wednesday." She elaborated: "Hilda had written a lovely new poem, rather on London and the raids, though without directly saying so, and she read it magnificently. The editor of the *Times L.S.* grabbed it for his paper and I'll try to send you a copy of it."[219] In her memoir, Bryher draws H.D. at this moment as "one of the Muses . . . speaking of the eternal conflict between wisdom and the world"; she claims that "it was H.D. who expressed more than any other writer the deeply felt but perhaps not always conscious feelings of the Londoners during the war."[220] The poem H.D. had read, published in the *Times Literary Supplement* on May 8, was "Ancient Wisdom Speaks to the Mountain," which features wisdom personified as a woman wearing a blue cloak. This persona speaks of the endurance of art and offers a prayer:

> *remember these* (you said)
> *who when the earth-quake shook their city,*
> *when angry blast and fire*
>
> *broke open their frail door,*
> *did not forget*
> *beauty.*[221]

The *Times* published an account of the reading itself, praising the revival of reading poetry aloud rather than relying on the page—difficult to do in wartime when paper was largely unavailable—and expressed a hope that even in the midst of war, lovers of poetry could form "a burning-glass through which . . . the whole English people catches alight and breathes the sacred fire of poetry," lofty words indeed but ones followed by a practical hope: "It can be said that the recital showed how enjoyable good reading can be—a useful lesson in times of long black-out. We may yet hear of reading aloud at A.R.P. [Air Raid Precautions] posts, at fire-watchers' posts, and during the recreation hour in the factories."[222]

Jubilant about the success of the event and her own performance—this occasion was H.D.'s first public reading—H.D. scrounged extra copies of the precious programs from Osbert and immediately sent them to American friends and relatives, to share the "heavenly revival of letters" across the ocean.[223] The event once again made poetry relevant, in a moment in which the practical reigned and art was neglected. In addition to the thrill of the reading itself, a week of parties surrounded the event, culminating in a reception hosted by Lady Crewe at the distinguished Argyle House in Chelsea. H.D. wrote Pearson, "We had such fun at the Reading of 'Famous Poets' (I ask you) that we forgot the war for a whole week and now I have got into a happy frame of mind and want to go on forgetting it—four years is too long!"[224] H.D. wrote Moore that "one almost feels that the war has stopped—in spite of the fact that since beginning this [letter], there has been a siren wailing."[225] Perdita described the reading as "all in all a most memorable event, a lovely splash in the dark bog of 1943, when it seemed the war would go on forever."[226] As momentous as this event was in the spring of 1943, its significance may have magnified in H.D.'s memory because history would prove that the headway the Allies were making would become permanent and lead to the end of the war—the tide was turning in 1943 with the German defeat at Stalingrad and the German and Italian surrender in North Africa.

The occasion also had its lighter moments, worth recounting briefly because they round out what were too often dismal years. One poet, Dorothy Wellesley, the duchess of Wellington also known as Lady Gerald Wellesley, was hilariously drunk. Before the reading, H.D. had been chatting with Sackville-West behind a chair, and when Lady Wellesley barged into their tête-à-tête, they shoved her out but, realizing how unsteady she was, stood her up and each took a side to make sure she remained standing. She did remain upright, even though she almost knelt while giving her reading.[227] According to Bryher, Lady Wellesley "was so much overcome by the occasion that she

had sipped rather too much cordial to appease her nerves. Various gentle-
men were making efforts to persuade her to retire but instead she turned on
one (so elderly, so respectable) and thinking it was Osbert, began to whack
him heartily with her stick. I watched entranced, knowing that I was unlikely
to be involved. People lost their heads, nobody knew what to do until Bea-
trice Lillie, dropping her programs, took control and led the lady firmly from
the aisle just before the solemn return of the regal procession."[228] H.D. had
her hair done for the event—in a permanent wave[229]—and was even able to
dress appropriately. According to Bryher, "Hilda fortunately had not used
her coupons"—a new dress required eight clothing coupons—"so was able
to have a new black dress for which they had the material and my mother's
little fur cape as it was very draughty on the platform. And a black beret."[230]

For H.D., "A Reading by Famous Poets" represented a turning point in
the war. As Osbert had hoped, it—joined with the advances the Allies were
making in the war—lifted everyone's spirits, and H.D. consequently wrote
the poem "May 1943," placed first in *What Do I Love?*, a poem that mingles
spring in London's Kensington Gardens with rationing in Britain and the
United States and the death of Goldie, the fair-haired ambulance driver.
"May 1943" was shortened, re-ordered, retitled as "Last Winter," and published in *Poetry* in December 1950, just as H.D. was sending her Christmas
volume *What Do I Love?* to friends.[231] At the time, Pearson was assiduously
working to find publication venues for H.D.'s work, and he was delighted
that the influential *Poetry* was interested in publishing this poem, even if the
editor insisted on altering it. So delighted was Pearson that he approved the
changes and the consequent proof without consulting H.D., a brash move
in which he rarely indulged. He wrote H.D. in November explaining the
changes editor Karl Shapiro asked to make: "Since [Shapiro] wanted it for
the December issue, and had to get the copy off to the printers for galleys, I
did an incredibly presumptuous thing and told him that it would be all right.
I am very anxious to have a poem of yours in POETRY, and I do see that
they are publishing a much much longer poem than is their wont, and so
are a little helpless in taking all. I daresay too that they have prior commit-
ments. Now, if you want to veto my approval send me a cable to that effect
and I will wire or phone him. But I hope you will agree with me." A December letter included the final publication details. Pearson assured her that the
poem "comes out wonderfully well, and I think you'll like it. I was only sorry
there wasn't time to get the proof to you. But as you know it is going into the
December number. Shapiro writes: 'We're leading off with this poem and

making it the main thing in the December issue.' Congratulations to you!"[232] Shapiro's interest underscores the poem's significance in the postwar period, and this publication history further clarifies H.D.'s relationship with Pearson.

The poem, told in thirteen sections, begins in Kensington Gardens at the orangery, the royal conservatory. The clock in the poem reads two o'clock, but it is only noon by the sun, the two-hour difference provided by double summer time. It is May 14, the trees are in blossom and leaf, and the persona is fifty-six, H.D.'s exact age.[233] H.D. writes that "the steps of William's orangery / at Kensington, / become the Venetian doge's water stair," likening the poem's setting in London to a staircase leading from the water to the Doge's Palace in Venice, another of her favorite cities (155). The direct inspiration for these lines can be found in a letter from H.D. to Osbert dated April 21, 1943: "I was so happy yesterday, sitting on the hot stones of the Orangery in Kensington gardens and scraping up branches from the walk under the half-pruned arches around the Dutch garden—and the chestnuts in flower—it was like Vienna or somewhere outside Florence or some eighteenth century garden off the lagoons beyond Padua—or where you will or London before the last war." She holds out this moment of pre–World War I peace and happiness that, when joined together with the "Reading of Famous Poets," becomes a "touch of the hem-of-the-garment of happiness" that she hopes will not be tarnished by more "despair and gloom and doom."[234] In her poem, the persona can "mend a break in time" with her pencil, just as the carpenter can mend a damaged window frame—probably from the bombing—with his chisel (155). The ability to mend extends to a sparrow—a creature whom God cares for, according to the Book of Matthew (10:29–31)—whose foot, caught in a flower root, is untangled by a person who has braved the gardener's wrath by leaping a locked gate in order to free the sparrow. The parallels between London and Venice continue, between canoes and gondolas, and the delicate items listed belong in Kensington Palace, in the Queen's Apartments, particularly her Drawing Room, to which the placard refers; it was indeed badly damaged by incendiary bombs on October 14, 1940. Spring in the gardens, coupled with the "Reading of Famous Poets," has offered hope: "I say the war is over . . . / the war is over" (157). The ideal of a world untouched by either war may be reachable, or at least this war-torn world may yet be healed and transformed back to its prewar state, a characteristically modernist statement which relies on the belief that a foundation exists and can be recovered.

But yet it was not, and the following ten sections establish two continuing realities of the war: rationing and death. H.D. quotes an American politician, a young brash politician from the west, who, when the United States is faced with rationing beginning in 1942, announces that "these people," that is, the British, "have the advantage over us," odd phrasing. Rationed food, peculiar clothes, limited furnishings, even "funny umbrellas" seem little advantage; instead, H.D. portrays Londoners as "a motley host, / dim, undistinguished, / water-rats / in the water, / land-rats in the gutter" (158). As the realities of rationing hit the United States, H.D. began receiving exasperating letters from Americans. She confided to Jordan that "a cousin from Cal[ifornia] wrote asking me if we had clothes rationed. All this has been going on with us for YEARS now and people only faintly catch-up."[235] Even Moore, who was well informed and had been sending H.D. and Bryher regular packages of food, seemed to lack a practical understanding of the consequences of rationing: "We are being noisily rationed, and threatened with involuntary rationing if we don't starve ourselves, & extend our wardrobes by discreditable expedients, without it . . . And it would be poltroonery to give the impression that we are short of food; the chief surprise is in high prices, and the doll-house amounts meted out for the customary money."[236] The dismal reality was "doll-house amounts," and H.D.'s reticence in sharing the reality of life in a besieged country became painfully clear. The poem's persona says, "yes, we're used to it, / we have the advantage, / you're new to it" and claims that the strength gained has made them heroic as they head "off to the bread-queue, / the meat-shop, the grocery, / an egg?—really madam—maybe tomorrow" (158–59).

This very ordinary type of civilian heroism is matched by Goldie's actions when she follows her orders and refuses to leave her post, even though that heroic action costs her life. Toward the poem's end, the Londoners' perseverance is interwoven with Goldie's, and together they become symbolic of the British determination to fight and persevere: "Goldie was one of us, / we are one with Goldie" (160). The London "rats" refuse to leave the sinking ship, "so the ship / didn't sink," the timber was true and solid (162). The poem closes on May 15 at 6:00 (4:00 by the sun) as the siren begins to wail again. The frogs have transformed into "salamanders in the flame, / heraldic wings surround the name / English," and Goldie, with the golden hair, has been transfigured into a princess or saint (163–64).

YOUR COURAGE
YOUR CHEERFULNESS
YOUR RESOLUTION

WILL BRING

US VICTORY

"Your Courage, Your Cheerfulness, Your Resolution Will Bring Us Victory,"
©Imperial War Museums (PST 14792).

This War Is Over, I Tell You

In 1944, the tide turned, but before good news arrived, there was more bad. Moore summed up the situation: "How this awful war drags on, killing and maiming so many fine boys. Sacrificing so many to rid the world of the German and Jap swine. Swine is too good a name for them. Pigs are useful but they are not. . . . I'm sorry to see by the papers that the Nazis are dropping bombs in England again. I wish the allies could down all their planes so they wouldn't be able to bomb any more."[237] The bombing of London had resumed. Friends' flats were destroyed, and terrific noise was again battering the city. The civilians, entering their fifth year of rationing and privations, were frightened and becoming bad tempered: "Nothing seems bearable," wrote Bryher. [238] In February, and again in March, Bryher wrote letters to Jordan describing the barrage:

> Well, we have had a perfectly awful week. Such a lot of our friends had their places damaged but mercifully were unhurt. But we are all suffering from a kind of concussion, they say it is partly due to our barrage, it is a great comfort to us but the noise is so terrific that it shocks the nerves of the head. The sky was magnificent, Hilda and I hung out of the window with all our lights off, and there were searchlights crossing like rapiers and great golden tassels of flares and what the populace has dubbed "the green chandelier" which we innocently supposed was our own stuff but the B.B.C. if I heard it rightly said was enemy, and dissolving red stars, anyway all flares and lights. One of the most strange and beautiful sights I have ever seen, and then suddenly, as one is feeling its complete irreality, a swish and a thump, and the whole great block rocks like a leaf, and one knows that somewhere people are killed and homeless.[239]

Surviving yet more bombing took a toll on the civilians, and rumors about a second front frayed nerves. On the continent, the Allies landed at Anzio in January; in February the Allies' bombing of Germany accelerated; and in June, Rome was captured.

D-Day was June 6, 1944; the Allies invaded occupied western Europe, beginning in Normandy—jubilant news that H.D. immediately included in letters. She wrote Jordan, "We have been almost too excited to live here with the news—I can't take it all in. We had bells from Normandy village last night on the radio. I imagine you get just about what we do—though possibly not, as they have established contact now with France and we are after all, so very near—alas, as we know to our cost."[240] She joined Bryher in sharing the news with American friends: "We all knew invasion was near but on Tuesday when it came, it wasn't in the morning papers or on the first news. . . . I rushed back, abandoning office to its fate, until I had heard the news flash at the hour but though we were all desperately excited, nobody seemed to be anything else but desperately calm."[241] In retrospect, Bryher wrote that this moment was anticlimactic:

> On June 6th I went to the bank in Sloane Street to get the weekly supply of petty cash. "It's started," the cashier said and although I had listened to the trucks passing at night for weeks, I wondered for a moment what he meant? We had had so many alarms and inconvenient surprises. "The Invasion," he added, noticing that I looked puzzled. I walked back to tell Hilda but there was no stir in the streets, many had still not heard the news, others could only think about the inevitable losses. Actually most Londoners were too battered by the raids to react at all. The Government, as usual, bungled the announcements. Naturally they could not tell us what was happening along the French coast but this had been a war directed against civilians as much as armies and instead of being determined and confident, they seemed to be apologetic about trying to end it.[242]

H.D., however, finds the silence soothing: "the news of the fall of Rome, followed up so soon after, by the Day or the D-Day doings, has so completely upset us all—we feel completely subdued, waiting, no excitement here; a very beautiful feeling, I think, people go into the open churches at noon-hour and just sit quietly, many young people. London seems almost un-cannily quiet—though there are occasional sweeps of the planes going out."[243] Both H.D. and Bryher desperately hoped for the liberation of France and news of Beach.

In retaliation, the Germans aimed new weapons at London. Rumors circulated about new bombs the Germans had in store for England, and soon the dangers of doodle-bugs, buzz-bombs, or fly-bombs—as these bombs were dubbed—became clear.[244] June 13 saw the first V-1 rocket launched at London, and the V-2 rockets took to the sky in September. The nicknames stemmed from the sound the rockets made, which Perdita describes: "In London the worst of times since the blitz, with its abominable robots, V's 1 and 2, flying bombs and rockets, falling indiscriminately where they would, twenty-four hours a day. The V 1's sounded variously like helicopters, lawn mowers, revved-up motorboats. The V 2's were more destructive, but descended without warning; at least we didn't have to monitor their progress across the sky. A disrupted city, inhabitants burrowing in like hysterical rabbits—just what Hitler had in mind. We went about our business as usual." Perdita goes on to provide an example of the three Sitwells standing firm in the face of these bombs: "They were assembled all three, Edith, Osbert, and Sashie, at the Churchill Club, a social and cultural center for Allied officers. Osbert had read and talked of a work in progress. Edith was on stage, reading a poem inspired by the 1940 bombings, 'Still Falls the Rain.' We heard *it* coming, the lawn mower variety, lower and lower and louder and louder, about to tear off the roof and chop down the staircase. Nobody flinched. Edith read on, raising her voice over the racket, modulating it as the thing continued on its way. That moment, and the applause that followed, has remained one of my personal highlights of the war."[245]

Despite Londoners' defiant attitudes, these capricious bombs forced them to retreat from public life. Tired of "dodging these shells or doodle-bugs," H.D. wrote Jordan, "in the big blitz or the old blitz (this is big enough but different) I went out a lot, was in cinemas and theatre and so on—but I am being more careful now. We simply go on and when possible, sit in the park in the sun—there has been mighty little of that. June simply was NOT. We had no June but now weather seems to be getting on to summer—and when fine the doodle-bugs lessen activity—at least, fewer get to London.[246] From June 13, 1944, to March 29, 1945, more than 8,000 V-1s were launched at London. British troops shot down many, but still about 2,400 hit targets in London, although the bombs decreased as German launch sites were eliminated by Allied troops. V-2s came into play from September 1944 till March 1945. These rockets caused thousands of civilian deaths as well as tens of thousands of injuries and destroyed more homes, including those of some of H.D.'s friends.

The fall brought positive developments: "at least, we see light now at the not-so-far end of the tunnel!" H.D. wrote to Wolle.[247] In August, Pearson, well informed through his position in the OSS, wrote to Bryher, "The weeks go quickly by, the soldiers march on through France, and before we know it Paris will be ours. Rome and Paris again out of German hands make torches into the dark sky. And nights are much quieter here as well. It is a good thing to keep away for a long while yet; who knows what the next night will bring in the way of new surprise of hell. But nevertheless it *is* easier, it is definitely easier."[248] On August 19, H.D. wrote to Jordan, "The news is terribly exciting. Last night, we heard on the wireless that the Battle of Normandy was won, and now, so soon, we will hear of Paris falling. It has all been a terrible strain and the long wait has worn us all down as we have been literally, the front-line for so long. I trust the doodle-bugs will cease from doodling but I don't think there is any guarantee of that even after France falls—as they may have moved them into Belgium or Holland . . . but anyhow, let us be thankful we have survived so far, and D.V.,[249] we will get through this last hard stretch, this last lap, I trust."[250]

On August 25, the Allies liberated Paris, and H.D. joyfully wrote to Dobson the next day: "I am so happy about France—I am standing on my head. The LIBERATION means so much to me and to Br[yher]—though to me especially, as it was to France I first went from USA before I saw England. Here, they are excited because it means victory and the war ending soon (D.V.) but to me it is something special and regenerating."[251] By October, H.D. and Bryher had heard that Sylvia Beach was safe and in Paris: "Now we are happy to hear for the first time from our dear friend Sylvia Beach who had the well-known book shop in Paris, she lectured too and was a great center for visiting English and people from USA, she is herself American. She had a dreadful time but she spares us and tells us how wonderful she thinks WE were in the blitz and later fly-bomb period—well, she was in Vittel, the concentration camp and we did NOT know how to get at her—finally heard indirectly via N.Y., and now at long last a letter from her. We feel so happy about it as she is free and fairly well."[252] The liberation of Paris and the freedom of Beach marked a shift in the war and foretold an Allied victory.

Christmas 1944 stood as a symbol of hope for a nation looking to rise from its bombed ashes. The stores offered nothing to buy for the holiday, but parcels arrived from American friends. Pearson came for Christmas dinner, and Perdita had four glorious days off, including Christmas Day, to spend with H.D. and Bryher. "Christmas 1944," the final poem in *What Do I Love?* opens with angels who have been disturbed by the war, just as the civilians have been. As the bombing gives Londoners the sensation of concussion, the communal persona in the poem is "dizzy and a little mad" because of the "experience of a world beyond our sphere" (173). The second, singular speaker wonders if the angels have been driven higher than the stratosphere by the bombs or if the angels have come to earth "to share our destiny" (173). As the sound of bombs beats on London, the speaker debates what the wait entails: a wait for death, to be remembered, to be forgiven, to rise to heaven, and she concludes that the question should be "what do I love?" (173).

This particular question is about objects: which of "all your loveliest treasures" one might choose to save (174). H.D. wrote Jordan about the July bombings: "I wanted to write about our raids, but never more than lightly touched on them. It's odd to walk down a familiar street and look up into a façade, open like a theater scene—and see a room open to the sky; at the top where a friend lived, where I visited her. . . . We live so very near death and the people who have gone from this city."[253] During July, friends Cole and Gerald Henderson's flat had been hit. Cole was away from home during the bombing, but Gerald—a librarian at St. Paul's who had survived the Blitz even when on watch as that church was ringed with fire—was blinded in one eye, and their flat was destroyed. Bryher described the bomb to Jordan: "Life here has been horrible, far worse than the big blitz I think. This morning I nearly died in the arms of a completely strange sailor and somehow I don't fancy that as my end! The danger overhead signal went and we both dived for the same bit of floor. A friend of ours was partially blinded and his flat wrecked two weeks ago. We have all had enough of it."[254] Into her memoir *The Days of Mars*, Bryher inscribed this incident and its aftermath. She and several other of their friends rounded up scarce boxes and headed for the Hendersons' flat. Given one hour in the ruined building to salvage what they could, the friends found the irreplaceable clothes, a saucepan, some china, and Cole's favorite fur hat; the jam collection, made with rationed sugar, could not be saved nor most of the furniture.[255] The individual speaker in "Christmas 1944" is faced with a similar question: Which treasure to save—a clock from the past and mere memory by now, a chunk of amber brought to her by a friend, painted swallows, a real cat? In the face of catastrophe, what does one save? How many items are allowed? What is *"too much?"* (175).

It is the third section of this poem that introduces the Christ child, a ray of hope for many during the war. Just as Christ was sent from the inn to the stable, the Hendersons and millions of others were left homeless. H.D. indicates that the loved items end up in a sacred place, a place of hope for the lost, and she closes the poem with hopes of forgiveness:

if we are dizzy
and a little mad,
forgive us, we have had
strange visitations
from the stratosphere. (176)

These lines frame the poem with hope and ask outsiders—those beyond the walls of London who have not lived with the angels during the bombings—for understanding. Herring, in his December 1944 editorial for *Life and Letters Today*, lamented the months of war still ahead, even though a German defeat was now inevitable. He wrote, "There would be more gaiety in our greetings were victory not still a 'long way off.' The long long trail goes a-winding, not with decent directness into the land of our dreams, but uphill, through fire and brimstone, through that famous wood whose trees defy its detection, through field, through briar, blood, sand, and all the other obstacles we are so obediently used to being called on to exult in."[256] A bittersweet prescience seems to inhabit both Herring's lines and H.D.'s poem; the civilian populace is definitely *"a little mad"* by this juncture in a long long war.

The new year brought increased hope—on one occasion in the form of ice cream. A local store was selling blocks of ice cream, and the simple pleasure of eating something different far outweighed the ice cream's inferior quality.[257] Hope came more practically in the accelerating invasion of Europe. Perdita, who had been working for the Americans, was in demand because of her languages, and her orders to go into the foreign service for the United States thrilled H.D. and Bryher. H.D. longed to share this good news with friends and, when she shared too many specifics in letters, cut the telling chunks out of the middle. In March she wrote to Jordan:

Perdita got her preliminary orders to go to "Europe"—more than that, I can not write, but you can imagine; it was a business saying goodbye a number of times and getting generally wrought up. Although her passport is British, she went in US uniform as she has been with the Embassy people here—the US—I am sure we told you. We could not see her actually off—as all the departure places etc. are kept secret and we have not heard from her yet—but members of her office and former colleagues are back and forth and I am sure, one day there will be a letter delivered personally by one of her pals. Her uniform, second Lieutenant, was so attractive and she had wonderful accessories, such as the girls here in the English services, don't dream of! Now she had an accumulation of clothes from five years back—and there are such a LOT of them. Cleaning problems are difficult, so she left many things half-and-half—and we have been seeing to them, and I assure you that I could go on living in her clothes for ten years—but I have been wrapping them up and putting them away, as for her future—D.V., it will be a happy one.[258]

Because of the continuing clothing shortage—Jordan had been sending clothes to them—H.D. did not dare give Perdita's things away. By April, Bryher wrote to Jordan that Perdita was having a wonderful time on the continent and greatly enjoying the American uniform and food and that Bryher had just been queuing for summer shoes.[259]

On May 19, 1945, H.D. wrote to Dobson, "A very happy PEACE to you!"[260] Events had accelerated: on April 28, Italian dictator Benito Mussolini was killed; on April 30, Hitler committed suicide with Eva Braun; on May 1, Goebbels killed himself; on May 7, the Germans surrendered unconditionally to the Allies. V-E Day, Victory in Europe, was celebrated on May 8, 1945. H.D. hung a huge American flag that covered her entire bedroom window; other windows in her flat sported British and Welsh flags. In Paris, Perdita reported, the RAF dropped sparkling flares and people were riotous,[261] but London was subdued and serene. Planes flying low to provide London views returned prisoners to their homeland, and the populace flowed into Trafalgar Square. H.D. and Bryher had a Victory tea with Herring, and they walked the streets, celebrating with all of London. In the evening, as Bryher recalls in her memoire, Pearson came to visit: "we celebrated by opening a tin of hoarded fruit juice, pulling back all the curtains and turning on the lights. It was the first time for almost six years."[262] Five years after H.D. wrote the hopeful line in "Before the Battle"—"This war is over, I tell you"—the war was over and spring arrived.

Notes

1. The subtitle phrase, "London, Capital of the Free World," appears in a letter H.D. wrote to Francis Wolle, November 8, 1941, H.D. Papers. Copies of H.D.'s letters to Wolle are held at the Beinecke; the originals are held by the University of Colorado Libraries.

2. Bryher, *The Days of Mars*, 115.

3. The most comprehensive list of H.D.'s composition and publication dates is Susan Stanford Friedman's "Chronology: Dating H.D.'s Writing," which can be found in her *Penelope's Web* (360–66).

4. Bryher, *The Days of Mars*, 116.

5. Because *Within the Walls* has been out of print and *What Do I Love?* has been largely unread as an intact volume, few scholars have written much directly about either text, but H.D. scholarship volubly discuses H.D. and war. Susan Schweik offers a rare scholarly analysis of *What Do I Love?*; see *A Gulf So Deeply Cut* for Schweik's fascinating argument about the Christmas theme in "Christmas 1944" and *Trilogy* (243–45). In her excellent scholarly book *The Persistence of Modernism*, Madelyn Detloff claims: "the compelling, apocalyptic language of *Trilogy* is not without its costs, however, for in its redemptive turn, the poem reinscribes loss as something triumphant, character-building, transformative" (80), which holds true throughout H.D.'s body of work. Detloff presents an interesting conundrum: is loss simply to be mourned, or should one try to focus on what it might produce? Is the phoenix metaphor always and only acceptance of the rhetoric of the nation-state, which needs to win, no matter the cost? On the one hand, then, H.D. did accept the national doctrine about war; however, Britain did not start the war—it resisted involvement for several years, and H.D. paid a huge personal price. Still, she found the war, with all of its costs, inspiring. She wrote to Mary Herr on February 8, 1944 (H.D. and Bryher Papers, Bryn Mawr College Library), "I have never worked so hard as in the past few years—a terrific creative urge that I suppose, is a sort of 'escapism' but a cerebral drug too, that has kept me sane and alive—the writing is crazy, if you will—but has acted as a sort of safety valve." Robert Duncan also offers an insightful analysis of H.D. as a war poet in *The H.D. Book*. He writes, "There was great work to undertake, but it was only in the experience of war-time London of the Second World War, where in the actual bombings life and death were so mixed, hope and despair, that the time ripened, the things of the poet's own inner life came due. The days of bombardment, the trials and crucible of the war, furnish a crucible of the poem where the long prepared art, the accumulated craft and knowledge fit or work. But it is the time too that fits, that works. In prophecy, this is the proof. It is the fulfilling of the word" (211). Marina Camboni glosses a few passages of *Within the Walls* in her analysis of *Trilogy*. For a reading of *Trilogy* as a war poem, see Sarah H. S. Graham's thorough article and Adalaide Morris's article on *Trilogy* as performing reconstruction; see also Scott Boehnen, Susan Edmunds (war and female aggression), Julie Goodspeed-Chadwick (war and trauma), and Walter Sutton (*Trilogy* and *The Pisan Cantos*). For an analysis of war, *Asphodel*, and *Bid Me to Live*, see Suzette A. Henke; see Elizabeth Willis on the atomic bomb, World War II, *Tribute to Freud*, and *Helen in Egypt*; see Miriam Fuchs and Victoria Harrison on war and *The Gift*. See also

Donna Krolik Hollenberg's important volume of letters between H.D. and Norman Holmes Pearson, whose friendship was cemented during World War II. See informative introductions in recent H.D. editions edited by Jane Augustine, Cynthia Hogue and Julie Vandivere, Demetres P. Tryphonopoulos, Lara Vetter, and Caroline Zilboorg. While not studies of war, Friedman's *Psyche Reborn* and *Penelope's Web* offer significant commentary on H.D. and war, as does Rachel Blau DuPlessis's *H.D. The Career of That Struggle*. For articles on teaching the theme of H.D. and war, see Raffaella Baccolini (*Trilogy*), Detloff's "Burnt Offerings or Incendiary Devices? Ambivalence, Trauma, and Cultural Work in *The Gift* and *Trilogy*," and Friedman's "Teaching *Trilogy*: H.D.'s War and Peace."

6. *Friends' Central News* from Overbrook, Pennsylvania, clipping dated January, 26, 1951, volume 20, number 5, H.D. Papers.

7. H.D. explained the publication of *What Do I Love?* to Pearson in her October 15, 1950 letter: "But Bryher and Robert had a tiny book set up, as for a Xmas card for me to send out, just before L. and L. folded up and they could put things through with the printer. I am posting you a pre-Xmas copy; it is just three poems, I think you have them, a series that I call May 1943, another I call R.A.F., the third and last, Christmas 1944. They hardly fit into any of the Trilogy sequences, but I like them and they do very well in this tiny book that I call 'What do I Love?' I have left the signature out, as I will sign the copies with Xmas greetings, I have 30 copies here; I think there are 50 altogether. I must ask Bryher" (Pearson Papers).

8. Bryher confided this plan to Pearson in her January 13, 1950 letter: "Hilda seems well and is preparing a sort of catalogue of her work. This should be very interesting. If L and L ceases as I fear it will next June, though no announcement will be made before late spring, I may get all of Hilda's unpublished poetry set up, just as it were, in galley form for reference. In no sense as even a booklet. We can have things set up in triplicate as if for use in the magazine at a reduced rate and I thought it would be handier for reference than scattered typescript and she likes the idea. But it is not certain that this can be done" (Pearson Papers).

9. H.D., "H.D. by Delia Alton," 203.

10. These poems are included in Louis L. Martz's *H.D. Collected Poems* at the end of the "Uncollected and Unpublished Poems" section in the order in which they were written; he may not have considered the private printing of these poems to be publication. In Friedman's "Chronology: Dating H.D.'s Writing," the publication date of *What Do I Love?* is given as 1944, which is incorrect; it was not printed until 1950. Several copies are held in Yale University libraries that include an inscription on the envelope in which they were sent; both inscriptions and envelopes are dated 1950. Letters confirm that date of printing.

11. Dobson, "Mirror for a Star," 289–90.

12. Bryher to Jordan, December 4, 1942, Jordan Papers.

13. The subtitle phrase, "Living on the Edge of a Volcano," comes from a letter written by H.D. to Clifford Howard, July 20, 1940, H.D. Papers.

14. H.D., *Tribute to Freud*, 58–59.

15. Bryher, *Heart to Artemis*, 276–85.

16. Dobson, "Mirror for a Star," 54.

17. This narrative is enclosed in a letter from Melitta Schmideberg to Perdita Schaffner, April 3, 1979, Barbara Guest Papers.

18. H.D. to Clifford Howard, September 23, 1939, H.D. Papers.

19. H.D. to Bryher, May 11, 1940, Bryher Papers.

20. See chapter 5 in Annette Debo's *The American H.D.* for a discussion of H.D.'s chosen family (192–203).

21. Herring, "Journal de Guerre," 1.

22. Ibid., 8.

23. H.D. to Bryher, June 2, June 5, and June 6, 1940, Bryher Papers.

24. H.D. to Bryher, June 3, 1940.

25. Delivered June 4, 1940.

26. H.D. to Bryher, June 5, June 6, and June 7, 1940, Bryher Papers.

27. A copy of this pamphlet is held in the Bryher Papers.

28. Moore to Bryher, March 17, 1940, Bryher Papers.

29. The subtitle phrase, "This Burning Light of Life," comes from a letter written by H.D. to Moore, June 27, 1940, Moore Papers.

30. H.D. to Bryher, July 16, 1940, Bryher Papers.

31. Moore to H.D., August 6, 1940, H.D. Papers.

32. H.D. to Bryher, August 13, 1940, Bryher Papers.

33. H.D. to Bryher, May 30, 1940.

34. Herring, "News Reel," vol. 26, 212.

35. Bryher to Jordan, January 30, 1944, Jordan Papers.

36. Bryher to Pearson, May 15, 1943, Pearson Papers.

37. H.D. to Bryher, May 21, 1940, Bryher Papers.

38. H.D. to Clifford Howard, September 26, 1940, H.D. Papers.

39. Perdita Schaffner's unpublished notes for a memoir held by the Schaffner family.

40. Bryher, *The Days of Mars*, 16.

41. Dobson, "Mirror for a Star," 85.

42. Bryher covers her journey in detail in *The Heart to Artemis*, 297–309.

43. H.D. to Moore, October 30, 1940, Moore Papers.

44. Moore to H.D., December 8, 1940, H.D. Papers.

45. H.D. to Moore, June 27, 1940, Moore Papers.

46. H.D. to Clifford Howard, September 26, 1940, H.D. Papers.

47. H.D. to Moore, October 30, 1940, Moore Papers.

48. Moore, *Selected Letters*, 400, 406.

49. Moore to H.D., December 28, 1940, H.D. Papers.

50. Farson, *Bomber's Moon*, 156.

51. H.D. to Francis Wolle, December 30, 1942, H.D. Papers.

52. Dobson, "Mirror for a Star," 328.

53. Herring, "News Reel," vol. 28, 112.

54. H.D. to Gretchen Wolle Baker, June 9, 1943, H.D. Papers.

55. H.D. to Gretchen Wolle Baker, February 14, 1941.

56. H.D. to Plank, January 7, 1941, Plank Papers.

57. H.D. to Gretchen Wolle Baker, February 14, 1941, H.D. Papers.

58. H.D. to Jordan, March 30, 1941, Jordan Papers.

59. H.D. to Jordan, May 5, 1941.

60. H.D., "H.D. by Delia Alton," 203.

61. H.D. to Jordan, October 5, 1941, Jordan Papers.

62. H.D. to Bryher, May 11, 1940, Bryher Papers.

63. Bryher to Jordan, January 18, 1942, Jordan Papers.

64. Moore, *Selected Letters*, 406.

65. Bryher to Clifford Howard, n.d., H.D. Papers.

66. Bryher to Moore, March 3, 1941, Moore Papers.

67. Bryher to H.D., January 25, 1941, H.D. Papers.

68. H.D. to Gretchen Wolle Baker, February 14, 1941, H.D. Papers.

69. H.D. to May Sarton, June 26, 1941, Berg Collection.

70. Bryher to H.D., January 25, 1941, H.D. Papers.

71. H.D. to Pearson, August 14, 1943, Pearson Papers.

72. Bryher, *The Days of Mars*, 12.

73. Schaffner, "Unless a Bomb Falls . . . ," ix.

74. Dobson, "Mirror for a Star," 297.

75. Perdita writes about Nefert, a real kitten H.D. and Bryher had when Perdita was little in Montreux, Switzerland, in her unpublished *Autobiography* (H.D. Papers). They lived in an immense white apartment house, #25, Riant Chateau that overlooked the lake, and they had two Siamese kittens, Nefert and Tiger (12).

76. H.D. to Francis Wolle, January 15, 1942, H.D. Papers.

77. H.D. to Jordan, July 30, 1944, Jordan Papers.

78. In a March 30, 1941 letter to Viola Jordan, H.D. explains that she is sending *Life and Letters Today*, which includes a piece "by 'voluntary worker' on driving mobile canteen, who is Perdita." H.D. again mentions this article in her April 24, 1941 letter to Jordan: "Did you get the copy with Perdita's article (the second canteen worker in the 2 articles on mobile canteens) unsigned?" Jordan Papers.

79. Perdita discusses her choices in her unpublished *Autobiography*, H.D. Papers.

80. H.D. to Clifford Howard, November 5, 1939, H.D. Papers.

81. Perdita Schaffner's unpublished notes for a memoir held by the Schaffner family.

82. Perdita Schaffner, "Canteen Backstage," 15–16, 15, and 21.

83. H.D. to Gretchen Wolle Baker, February 14, 1941, H.D. Papers. H.D. also shares Perdita's plans with Jordan in a letter incorrectly dated February 14, 1944, Jordan Papers; it should be dated 1941 based on the references to Perdita's forthcoming article in *Life and Letters Today*.

84. H.D., "A Letter from England," 22.

85. Perdita to H.D., June 1, 1941, H.D. Papers.

86. Bryher to H.D., May 31, 1941, H.D. Papers.

87. Pearson to H.D., July 9, 1943, H.D. Papers.

88. Quoted in H.D. to Pearson, August 14, 1943, Pearson Papers.

89. See Debo, *The American H.D.*, for a discussion of Perdita's OSS work (chapter 2).

90. H.D. wrote to Bryher on September 7, 1940, "A radio commentator said something I have felt and said to myself for a long time. We are on a SHIP. That is what it is. The island IS a ship—and things going on, on 'land' as it were (America) are simply out of another element—especially when ship is in storm." See Bryher Papers.

91. Halsey, *With Malice toward Some*, 93.

92. Herring, "Editorial," vol. 34, 155.

93. H.D. to Clifford Howard, September 26, 1940, H.D. Papers.

94. See Friedman, *Analyzing Freud*, 241, 276.

95. *J'Accuse!* 12, 13.

96. H.D. to Jordan, January 6, 1945, Jordan Papers.

97. Bryher to Moore, August 23, 1940, Moore Papers.

98. H.D. to Jordan, March 25, [no year given but probably 1942]; May 5, 1941; July 28, 1942; July 5, 1943, Jordan Papers.

99. Bryher to Jordan, July 29, 1942, Jordan Papers.

100. Beach's account was written between 1959 and 1962 and published only in 2009.

101. Bryher to Moore, December 15, 1964, Moore Papers.

102. Schaffner, "A Day at the St. Regis," 114.

103. Bryher, *The Days of Mars*, 18.

104. Bryher to Moore, March 3, 1941, Moore Papers.

105. Edith Sitwell to Bryher, June 13, 1941, Bryher Papers.

106. H.D. to Jordan, April 9, 1944, Jordan Papers.

107. Bryher to Jordan, 2 June 1944, Jordan Papers.

108. Dobson, "Why Bulldoze Xanadu?" 205.

109. H.D. to May Sarton, May 8, 1941, Berg Collection.

110. H.D., "H.D. by Delia Alton," 203.

111. H.D. to Bryher, August 6, 1940, Bryher Papers.

112. Kenneth Macpherson to H.D., incorrectly dated June 15, 1943, H.D. Papers. Internal evidence indicates that the letter should be dated 1940.

113. H.D. to Bryher, July 20 and August 6, 1940, Bryher Papers.

114. Bryher to H.D., August 15, 1940, H.D. Papers.

115. Bryher to H.D., January 25, 1941, H.D. Papers.

116. H.D. to Jordan, May 18, 1945, Jordan Papers.

117. H.D. to Perdita, April 1, 1950, held by the Schaffner family.

118. Bryher to H.D., September 29, 1950, H.D. Papers.

119. H.D. to Perdita, June 22, 1950, held by the Schaffner family.

120. H.D., "A Letter from England," 22.

121. Ibid.

122. Dobson, "Mirror for a Star," 294. The subtitle phrase, "Remain You Our Goddess of Raids," appears in a letter from Robert Herring to H.D., July 10, 1951, H.D. Papers.

123. Moore to Marshall A. Best of Viking Press, May 11, 1941, H.D. Papers.

124. H.D. to Bryher, June 2, 1940, Bryher Papers.

125. H.D. to Jordan, June 30, 1941, Jordan Papers.

126. H.D. to Herr, July 31, 1941, H.D. and Bryher Papers, Bryn Mawr College Library.

127. H.D. to Bryher, July 30, 1941, Bryher Papers.

128. Bryher to H.D., August 5, 1941, H.D. Papers.

129. Herring, "Editorial," vol. 33, 140.

130. H.D. to Bryher, September 18, 1941, Bryher Papers. H.D. also mentions this experience in *Compassionate Friendship* (H.D., *Magic Mirror*, 108), affirming that it happened in September 1941 on her return from Cornwall.

131. H.D. to May Sarton, March 2, 1942, Berg Collection.

132. Henrey, *The Incredible City*, 132. Madeline Henrey wrote under the pseudonym Robert Henrey, her husband's name, and this book is part of her London trilogy.

133. Ibid., 97, 156.

134. H.D. to Jordan, November 10, 1941, Jordan Papers.

135. H.D. to Herr, November 9, 1941, H.D. and Bryher Papers, Bryn Mawr College Library.

136. H. D. to Clifford Howard, April 28, 1942, H. D. Papers.

137. Herring, "Editorial," vol. 32, 1.

138. Pollard, *You and the Call-Up*, 4.

139. Ibid., 5.

140. Ibid., 10.

141. Ibid., 25.

142. Bryher to Jordan, November 12, 1943, Jordan Papers.

143. Pollard, *You and the Call-Up*, 32.

144. H.D. to Hattie Howard, July 13, 1942, H.D. Papers.

145. H.D. to Bryher, August 5, 1942, Bryher Papers.

146. Bryher to Jordan, July 29, 1942, and July 26, 1943, Jordan Papers.

147. Bryher to H.D., May 20, 1940, H.D. Papers.

148. Dobson, "Mirror for a Star," 290.

149. Ibid., 348.

150. H.D. to Bryher, August 19, 1942, and Thursday 12:30, [n.d. but probably written during H.D.'s annual August visit] 1944, Bryher Papers.

151. Dobson, "Mirror for a Star," 360.

152. Quoted in Kramer, *Land Girls*, 15.

153. Ibid., 77, xx.

154. Silvia Dobson's relationship with H.D. was not without conflicts. Dobson and H.D. were lovers briefly in the 1930s, and for H.D., this relationship was fleeting and smoothly segued into one of friendship. For Dobson, however, this relationship was formative, and for decades she longed to recapture it, often dwelling on the Easter she spent with H.D. in Venice. H.D., Bryher, Macpherson, and Herring fended off Dobson's efforts to be part of their familial network, relegating her to the periphery; she was an aspiring writer who never succeeded as one; and she accepted but resented Bryher's many financial gifts, which, after clever investment, allowed her to live comfortably for the rest of her life. A mixture of unrequited desire, resentment, and grudging gratitude clouds her reminiscences. Still, her memories of the time and H.D. remain valuable. "Mirror for a

Star. Star for a Mirror" is a memoir consisting of letters H.D. wrote to Dobson and Dobson's reminiscences. Dobson excerpted from this manuscript in her article "'Shock Knit within Terror': Living through World War II." "Why Bulldoze Xanadu?" is Dobson's life story. Dobson's efforts to publish either never bore fruit, but she did provide the bulk of the financial support for the H.D. Fellowship at the Beinecke, a tangible way to encourage H.D. studies.

155. H.D. to Clifford Howard, September 26, 1940, H.D. Papers.

156. Dobson, "Mirror for a Star," 280.

157. Dobson, "Why Bulldoze Xanadu?" 168.

158. The nickname could refer to any of the broadcasters but generally referred to the most prominent, William Joyce.

159. Dobson, "Why Bulldoze Xanadu?" 169.

160. Dobson, "Mirror for a Star," 281.

161. Ibid., 282.

162. Dobson, "Why Bulldoze Xanadu?" 170, 171, 173.

163. Dobson, "Mirror for a Star," 313–14, 325.

164. Bryher to H.D., May 20, 1941, H.D. Papers.

165. See Debo's *The American H.D.* (chapter 2) for an analysis of what it meant to be an American writer during the Cold War and Pearson's involvement in H.D.'s position in the American literary canon.

166. See Hogue and Vandivere's introduction to H.D.'s *The Sword Went Out to Sea: (Synthesis of a Dream), by Delia Alton.* They claim that the visions in that text are "highly selective accounts of what were actual hallucinations that H.D. experienced . . . which include the story of the destruction of London around St. Paul's Cathedral by a small atom bomb" (xxxiv).

167. Perdita Schaffner to Bryher, March 22 and April 17, 1946, Bryher Papers.

168. Bryher to Jordan, June 7, 1946, Jordan Papers.

169. Bryher to Jordan, December 7, 1946, Jordan Papers; H. D. to Jordan, July 5, 1943, Jordan Papers.

170. Bryher to Jordan, June 7, 1946, Jordan Papers.

171. Bryher to Francis Wolle, March 20, 1946, Bryher Papers.

172. Perdita Schaffner to Bryher, June 20, 1946, Bryher Papers.

173. H.D. to Pearson, September 26, 1946, Pearson Papers.

174. Bryher to H.D., September 29, 1946, H.D. Papers.

175. H.D. to Pearson, September 29 and October 22, 1946, Pearson Papers.

176. Herring, "Editorial," vol. 48, 154.

177. Bryher, *The Days of Mars,* 27.

178. H.D. to Jordan, January 28, 1943, Jordan Papers.

179. Bryher to Jordan, January 13, 1943, Jordan Papers.

180. Bryher to Jordan, October 12, 1944, and October 18, 1942.

181. H.D. to Gretchen Wolle Baker, April 29, 1944, H.D. Papers.

182. Bryher to Jordan, February 1, 1942, Jordan Papers.

183. Bryher, *The Days of Mars,* 10.

184. H. D. to Jordan, July 4, 1942, Jordan Papers.

185. Bryher to Jordan, February 1, 1942, Jordan Papers.

186. Bryher to Jordan, February 20 and April 4, 1942.

187. Herring, "Editorial," vol. 44, 121–24.

188. Bryher to Jordan, November 12, 1943, Jordan Papers.

189. Bryher, *The Days of Mars*, 5.

190. These clippings are of unidentifiable origin because they are clipped so narrowly. Held in Bryher Papers.

191. Bryher to Jordan, February 20, 1942, Jordan Papers.

192. H. D. to Jordan, July 4, 1942, Jordan Papers.

193. Bryher to Jordan, May 29, 1943, Jordan Papers.

194. Bryher to Jordan, April 25, 1942, Jordan Papers.

195. Bryher to Jordan, October 12, 1944, Jordan Papers.

196. Bryher to Jordan, October 12, 1994, Jordan Papers.

197. H.D. to Bryher, July 31, 1941, Bryher Papers.

198. Bryher to Jordan, December 4, 1942, Jordan Papers.

199. H.D. to Jordan, November 28, 1942, Jordan Papers.

200. Bryher to Moore, December 25, 1942, Moore Papers.

201. Bryher to Jordan, July 5, 1943, and January 18, 1942, Jordan Papers.

202. H.D. to Gretchen Wolle Baker, January 4, 1942, H.D. Papers.

203. Bryher to Pearson, n.d., Pearson Papers.

204. H.D. to Beach, n.d. but probably 1944, H.D. Papers.

205. Beach to Bryher, December 11, 1944, Bryher Papers.

206. CARE, "History of CARE."

207. Beach to Bryher, September 3, 1948, Bryher Papers.

208. Beach to Bryher, February 12, 1946.

209. H.D. to Jordan, October 31, 1943, Jordan Papers.

210. H. D. to Francis Wolle, November 16, 1942, H.D. Papers.

211. Bryher to Jordan, February 14, 1943, Jordan Papers.

212. Bryher to Jordan, October 22, 1943 and January 9, 1944, Jordan Papers.

213. H.D. to Gretchen Wolle Baker, April 2, 1944, H.D. Papers.

214. Bryher to Jordan, June 11, 1944, and February 14, 1943, Jordan Papers.

215. Also reading were Edmund Blunden, Gordon Bottomley, Wilfrid Gibson, W. J. Turner, Arthur Waley, and Dorothy Wellesley. Laurence Binyon was listed on the program but passed away in March, so his poems were read by Masefield.

216. Bryher to Moore, April 18, 1943, Moore Papers.

217. H. D. to Francis Wolle, April 26, 1943, H.D. Papers.

218. Herring, "Editorial," vol. 37, 55, 54.

219. Bryher to Moore, April 18, 1943, Moore Papers.

220. Bryher, *The Days of Mars*, 83, 84.

221. H.D., *Collected Poems*, 482.

222. "The Poets Speak," 187.

223. H. D. to Moore, April 18, 1943, Moore Papers.

224. H. D. to Pearson, May 2, 1943, Pearson Papers.

225. H. D. to Moore, April 18, 1943, Moore Papers.

226. Schaffner, "A Day at the St. Regis," 116.

227. H.D. to Osbert Sitwell, April 21, 1943, H.D. Papers. Copies of H.D.'s letters to Sitwell are held at the Beinecke; the originals are held by the Harry Ransom Center at the University of Texas at Austin.

228. Bryher, *The Days of Mars*, 87.

229. H.D. to Gretchen Wolle Baker, May 11, 1943, H.D. Papers.

230. Bryher to Moore, April 18, 1943, Moore Papers.

231. Pearson received a package of manuscripts including *What Do I Love?* from H.D., and he wrote her a letter confirming that they arrived on December 2, 1950.

232. Pearson to H.D., October 20 and November 5, 1950, H.D. Papers.

233. Christine Battersby pointed out to me that on the dates mentioned in the poem, May 14 and 15, Pearson wrote H.D. and H.D. responded (Hollenberg, *Between History and Poetry*, 23–26). Pearson's May 14 letter mentions the Allies' victory in Tunisia, a hopeful development he equates with the rebirth of spring, and Hollenberg's note references a May 13, 1943, headline in the *New York Times*: "African War Over" (61, n30). The article begins "The war in Africa is over, it was officially announced tonight" (Kluckhohn, "African War Over," 1), a line H.D. may be echoing in her own lines "I say the war is over . . . / the war is over" (157).

234. H.D. to Osbert Sitwell, April 21, 1943, H.D. Papers.

235. H.D. to Jordan, January 28, 1943, Jordan Papers.

236. Moore to H.D., October 8, 1942, H.D. Papers.

237. Ibid., January 25, 1944.

238. Bryher to Jordon, May 2, 1944, Jordon Papers.

239. Bryher to Jordan, February 27, 1944, Jordan Papers.

240. H. D. to Jordan, June 16, 1944, Jordan Papers.

241. Bryher to Jordan, June 11, 1944, Jordan Papers.

242. Bryher, *The Days of Mars*, 130–31.

243. H.D. to Francis Wolle, June 10, 1944, H.D. Papers.

244. H.D. to Francis Wolle, April 10, 1945.

245. Schaffner, "A Day at the St. Regis," 116.

246. H.D. to Jordan, July 17 and July 8, 1944, Jordan Papers.

247. H.D. to Francis Wolle, November 9, 1944, H.D. Papers.

248. Pearson to Bryher, August 12, 1944, Pearson Papers.

249. D.V. is an abbreviation H.D. often used; it stands for the Latin term *Deo Volente*, or God willing.

250. H.D. to Jordan, August 19, 1944, Jordan Papers.

251. H.D. to Dobson, August 26, 1944, Dobson, "Mirror for a Star."

252. H.D. to Jordan, October 13, 1944, Jordan Papers.

253. H.D. to Jordan, July 30, 1944, Jordan Papers.

254. Bryher to Jordan, July 17, 1944, Jordan Papers.

255. Bryher, *The Days of Mars*, 134–40.

256. Herring, "Editorial," vol. 43, 121.

257. Bryher to Jordan, February 11, 1945, Jordan Papers.

258. H.D. to Jordan, March 25, 1945, Jordan Papers.

259. Bryher to Jordan, April 18, 1945, Jordan Papers.

260. H.D. to Dobson, May 19, 1945, Dobson, "Mirror for a Star."

261. H.D. to Dobson, May 16, 1945, Dobson, "Mirror for a Star."

262. Bryher, *The Days of Mars*, 161.

Within the Walls

꩜ ꩜ ꩜

H.D.

Within the Walls

(January 1941)

The whole conception of time must be re-valued. To me, this day has its special significance, for all of us, within the walls, it is first and foremost a quiet day after an un-bombed night. That in itself sets it apart, sets us in another time sequence. Those without the walls, *extra muros*, even here in England, have already separated themselves or mercifully perhaps, been separated, from this particular crowd, that has endured for such a long time, at such intensity, unprepared (as certain Eastern peoples, by their very fatalism are prepared) to meet the eventuality of death. Simple people, dull, many villainous at heart, hypocrites, granted, yet there is the difference, there are those *extra muros* and those *intra muros*.

We enter life, observe, feel. Bee met a former Bloomsbury intellectual, now turned warden in the pioneer corps; he had been working in a demolition sector and remarked that for his part, he considered that the horrors of being buried alive, for him at least were mitigated by the fact that death came suddenly, and when it did not come, for the most part, the rescued were hearty and happy, probably simply glad to be alive. He said there seemed to be little of the in-between states, either you were killed outright or cushioned in the debris, with air of sorts to breathe. He felt that so far, those rescued, were amazingly balanced; weak, shaken, of course, but with notable exceptions, as a rule, after a brief time to recuperate and rest, they continued their normal round.

N., whom we knew in Geneva, turned up. An officer in the Dardanelles in the last war, he was amusing and seemed amused by the fact that he was again to wear khaki, to "go back to school." He chatted with the girl, also now called up for training with her Ambulance unit. She has been driving the mobile canteen, while waiting for this job. N. said he thought we had had, in town, as bad as the Nazis could give us, or we would have had it worse. That seemed comforting logic. We discussed the various time-bombs and land-mines of the immediate vicinity. The girl of course, highly professional, told us if there was one, there was bound to be a second, as they dropped one from each wing.

– – – – –

January 14, 1941 is different, each day is different, has its peculiar timbre or quality. This of course, obviously, may be said of any day, at any time. But we do not notice separate days unless they are days of some peculiar personal significance, a birth-day or some anniversary. Every day is a birth-day, an anniversary. Hour is cut from hour in precious prismatic fragments, the whole at the end, is a whole day, which might have been a part-day. An extra day has been given us, January 14, 1941.

January 14, 1941 is like a window miraculously unbroken in a house holding firm above the earthquake. As our personal house of life is threatened, we appreciate each hour. To-day especially we seemed to meet and smile at some secret. We have a secret. We are alive. Almost, the voice of the turtle is heard in the land.

– – – – –

Within the walls, we are within the walls of our own bodies, for the time being. This is a notable experience.

Bunny

(January 1941)

Can it be true that actually there is a girl of 19, called Bunny Thunder, with whom my own child yesterday and Saturday, drove, in a huge mobile canteen, into the devastated city?

"How did you manage to get in?" I asked her at tea-time, remembering our own journey through traffic-jams and bottle-necks, back from Liverpool Street Station this morning. "O, they let *us* through," she said, "past the dynamite and demolition squads and everything." "O—ye-es—and Bunny Thunder? if that really is her name—" "O—Thunder is. Her first name is Bertha or Bertina or something like that, she hates it—" "Of course. So they just call her Bunny—with the Thunder—a slight contradiction, I mean, in terms—" saying anything in an inane way, just to carry myself over the emotion, to bridge across this chasm, just to be ordinary, for that surely is what they need, if these child Valkyries need anything of their somewhat astonished and not a little shattered mothers.

But the girl does not appear to notice any gap or gasp and chats on in her breezy fashion, as if there were no chasm (and possibly there is no chasm) for which any bridge of words is needed. She needs no bridge. She springs with winged heels. "I asked Bunny to spend the night last night, as it was her night off." "O, that was nice—" "But she said she never took her night-off, she might miss something." "I see. They must have been pretty busy, what with this and what with that," being inane, "this week-end." "Yes. But she gets tired, she says, waiting for the night and things to happen at her fire-station, and asks for day-work. That's how she happened to be sent along to help me with my van."

– – – – –

So have you anything to say? I haven't. I have nothing to say who would say a great deal; whatever I say would not, can not touch the core of my real meaning. Words may wrap round a sentiment, a flame, but I can not put into prose or poetry—who can?—just this, "she gets tired waiting for the night-bombing, so she asked for day-work and they sent her to my van. She wears blue pants." A girl called Bunny in blue pants! "Tough?" I murmur, "a little bit on the tough side?" I mean it in admiration; the girl knows what I mean; her eyes quirk shut in her sort of way of answering a smile, "it's funny, you'd think she'd look tough, but she has curls pushed under a cap."

O, I dare say, I dare say, I dare say. One might have been spared the curls under the cap. We are spared nothing.

"A little tough—Bunny?" We understand, we of the inner circle. I would rather a flaming wall did not totter down on that particular mobile canteen. And that means, that, just that. Do you without the walls, know what this means? Why try to get across anything, in words? You may find words for this, when this is over. But we watch them as they stride across barriers, marked clear for all to read, no admission, dangerous, land-mine or time-bomb or just demolition squad and dynamite.

They are pushing out the borders, they enter the inner rim, not in any "feminine rights" manner, but in some heroic way that has nothing to do with their blue pants, they take them pretty much for granted. The blue pants and those pretty legs, they walk in and through the flames, they have crossed the circle. Outside in life, every day, all day, in the black night, all night, those pretty feet are pushing forward in a new dance, a cosmic dance of heroism, such as the world has never seen nor dreamed of.

Pattern

In my dream, I have been sleeping in a comfortable little bungalow, away from home. It is not far from my own home, about twenty minutes walk. I walk home and find my mother in a small house, a cosy room. As if I and my mother lived alone together. Actually in my life, we were seldom alone together, there was an enormous family, visiting relatives and friends. My mother is actually my mother. This is more miraculous than any divine manifestation. I am troubled because I have left my little travelling clock in this bungalow where I had been sleeping. I will go back for it, my mother says, "no, you are not to go back."

Now, my mother is showing me a piece of tapestry. It is apparently my own. I am not satisfied with it, but "see," she says, "the pattern is not broken." I am sure the stitching is slip-shod and badly done but she says, "no, look, there is the one line running through it all." There is a somewhat vague tapestry edge to the centre picture. I do not see the picture. We are concerned with the border. It is a wave pattern, the curves meet and run along symmetrically the whole length. Then the wave pattern seems to dissolve or resolve into fleur-de-lys. The last two flower-heads in their separate sections are done most carefully; they are clearer and firmer than the rest and beautifully finished. "Look," my mother says, "the pattern runs right to the end," as if she wanted to assure me that the pattern of my life was right, that the thread would not be cut abruptly, that I was weaving toward an established end.

My mother is satisfied, pleased with my work and now I find by some miracle, the little clock has come back, it is there, ticking away.

Dream of a Book

(January 1941)

This race with time—who is going to win? There are already 40,000 civilian casualties. The people downstairs, turn on the radio or the radio-gram with a series of somewhat out-of-date American swing records. Their little dog yaps and they shout to one another through the rooms. Bee in the other bed-room, across the hall-corridor, shouts across to me about eleven, "cheer up, they usually stop about one."

I can not listen, I can not not-listen. If I could get up and type in the middle of the night, I would do so. If I read too late or type, my eyes are tired, blurred in the morning; I can not read any more, I must read some hours every day, it is food. But perhaps in all this turn-over, my nerves will turn over, my eyes get a new strength. Anyway, I did get up and plug my ears with wax and suddenly, the inside of my head was quiet and I was listening as it were to snow falling. It was as quiet as that.

I was happy, in a familiar dimension. So far, I have not plugged my ears, not even in the worst gun-fire. It seemed safer to hear what was going on, even though my head felt like an eggshell about to crack. We are tougher than we know. One ear started to bleed, after one of the blitz-nights, but even so, I could not bear to shut out sound.

Now I believe, I will be able to plug out the sound with the balls of wax; it will give me a new dimension. Doctors advise us to do this; one doctor told me that he had the greatest difficulty with his women patients, men would follow his directions, but not one woman in ten. Early in the Blitz, the government advised official ear-plugs. I bought these wax-balls some time ago, but could never bear to use them.

My chief concern and worry is about my writing. I try to go over the stacks and heaps of old MSS I have collected and put aside, but I can not work any of it into shape; it is to me, dead wood. If I am not blitzed, of course it may be interesting, in some years time, to shape some of the old stuff, but now it is, as I say, perfectly dead. I can not decently bury it; I destroy certain papers, but then I say to myself, after all, if I am blitzed, the house will go with me and the stack of papers will go, too. This, that I now write will go with it, and why does one type pages that only have the slightest chance of survival? I asked myself that, last night, with that acute sense of silence.

Then, in that soft *sound* of silence, I asked myself again, as I have a thousand times, why I should worry and what does it matter? If I am blitzed, I won't care what people make of my old pages and anyway they will be blitzed with me. But there was another answer in that silence, as of snow falling on snow.

I have had through the years, dreams of a book, a book that I have written. But this writing would merge, like pictures in a picture-book, into dreams. I have written down some of those dreams, as they occurred during the years, but I can't now (racing with time) look out the old notebooks and re-type the dreams. But the substance of the dream was the book, over and over. But this book had to be alive, that is what it was. The papers that I turn over, in the light of that dream-book are dead. Pages I type at random, are not my conception of a book. I must let go my critical faculty, I can not afford to criticize or re-consider these words. They are the words of the spell; no matter how haphazard, how apparently unrelated, how profuse, how illogical, they are the words that in a sense—this is what it is—*keep me alive.*

Obviously, this book, this spell-book must be related to my first book, my first spelling-book. The book to live, must go back to the first book, the first spell or spell-ing. We all forgot our first book. We went off at various tangents and writing went dead. We must get back to the first spell-ing book and the magic of making pictures in one's head before one could spell. The real spell must relate and derive from the pre-spelling book days.

– – – – –

Now the girl comes in and we all have morning coffee together. She was amused by a letter I had this morning. "I think," George writes, "that she is marvellous; she wrote me a delightful letter in which she said she was so thankful she did not go to the U.S., that she realizes she is living life with a big L. I think it is wonderful the way these darling young things leap into the heart of the Fray, and it is the duty of all of us old things after the Chaos of Peace arrives to help THEM to form a world decent enough for them to live in. The Old Predatory Spiders must be exterminated."

Escape

(January 1941)

Last night, I could shake and quake; I could let myself shiver in bed; it was cold enough admittedly and as well, I had seen a film in the afternoon "Escape," the theme of which has been long familiar to my immediate circle of friends.

The average person is amazed and surprised by stories of the concentration camps. The newspapers only now begin to hint at the depth of depravity. I quote from *I Accuse*. "The enormity and ferocity of these tortures are almost beyond belief."

Then one must forget; poignant sympathy for refugees and various victims has been drained dry; one is forced to harden oneself, or cease living altogether.

Then I see a film, "Escape," and a new character is given to the news-reels that follow; the news-reels become fictitious, these are London fires and Hollywood horrors. "Escape" is a romance, a story, it is true, but I, in life, walk straight out of the Empire Theatre, Leicester Square into a snowy street scene. Real snow lies on the pavement, real snow powders the trees and does not drip off almost at the moment of settling; snow is so rare in London, that this Square and this street became completely unreal. Yes, this is Leicester Square, but my eyes have been adjusted to the film-sequence and there was snow in many of those sets. I walk into a film-set and as I push my way through the late afternoon crowd waiting for admission, toward a taxi that is just depositing its passengers, the film-set, this unreal scene has its very real sound going on.

It is not just that the talk and laughter of people is a little different, against the background of the soft snow and that the cab wheels are muffled in the snow; individual voices are clearer, more like sound-effects, because the rumble of the traffic is softened. But there is another sound, real movie-sound, war-sound. It is as if the news-reel had got mixed up with the romance, that we were listening to sound-effects in another studio, not meant for us. Or are they meant for us?

I was hesitating as to whether to allow myself the luxury of the taxi, but this settled it; there was the taxi and I was first to engage the cabman while the last passenger was looking for his change.

A little spurt of laughter answered the sound, from a group by the box-office; "time-bombs" was what they were saying, "it's exploding time-bombs." Without warning, no sound of siren, here was this news-reel gun-fire going on so very near, above or in the thick blanket of snow, and the snow fell just the same; obviously a mistake was being made. "Snow-fall" was being mis-read by some somewhat groggy stage-manager for "gun-fire."

Now I would take the taxi anyway, if it would take me. Blocked in that soft fall of snow before Piccadilly Circus, my man leans out and jokes with a neighbouring driver. "They didn't give us no warning," was what he said, as if this was a great joke, a little extra and a surprise at that.

— — — — —

The dream-state, the romantic 4th dimensional stage or screen condition of mind, the art-dimension, as it were, the actual life dimension or actual re-alities of life all merge and flow along together. Probably terror deeply felt in childhood, submerged terror or half-submerged, is tapped by this supreme terror that is always with us. Tales in fairy-books or a chance glimpse of illus-trations in The Book of Martyrs or some picture from our illustrated Gustav Doré bible or the Ancient Mariner which we spread open, before we could read, on our grandmother's carpet, seared deeply, awakened one's mind to the actual reality of death.

What was not fully understood—and no one does ever fully under-stand—was tactfully slurred over; "what is this, in the Ancient Mariner?" "O, it's some spirits, angels." "And this skeleton?" They could not say, "that is Death." They say, "O, it's just a picture in a book." The pictures remain after later reading is forgotten. If we can find the suitable incantation we can ban-ish the terror. What is the answering spell? How can we banish what is so deeply hidden, seared in consciousness and then walled over like the prover-bial fly in amber or the erring nun, immured for eternity within her wall?

It was something that might come when one went to sleep. It was part and parcel of "and if I die before I wake, I pray the Lord, my soul to take."

Who is this Lord we pray to? I tried to find Him last night, shivering in bed. Holy Wisdom was too abstract, there is no answer that Wisdom can give at this moment. What is it that I am afraid of? Well, before the night is over I may be caught in a blaze of falling timbers, be burnt (out of the Book of Martyrs) to death. But we must not think of being burnt to death. The Book of Martyrs disappeared, along with the pictures in the Ancient Mariner.

It is the unseen, the unrealized, the deeply immured image that is the most dangerous. This present shock may crack the wall of an old immured shock.

Why am I afraid? Why do I shake in the dark? I have had four months of constant blitz and to-day I was happy, coming home in the snow, with the taxi-driver leaning out of his cab and joking with his neighbour, "they didn't give us no warning, this time."

No warning, that is it—from what is it, good-Lord-deliver-us? From something and something and sudden death. What can I say? I will say something. I must find some words, I must dispel the terror, I must lay the ghost, I must abracadabra-ize something.

Blue Lights

(January 1941)

I tangled myself in the cord of my reading-lamp, a major tragedy, last night but this morning Louisa herself unscrews the cap and mends it. It is working again. My hot-water bottle also leaked, but thanks to the Nazis for once, I was wakened before too great damage was done to my blankets. If two things break, three will; Jo used to say, "there is an old charwoman or gypsy idea that if you yourself break the third, you will lay the spell—a match-stick will do." I fumble for a match-box in the dark and break a fresh match-stick, *eureka*, now we are finished for to-night, last night. My house even, may come under this sanction—anyhow, the raiders did not stay very long.

Bee who is "always right," alas, goes on and on about the great blitz due in March. She wants me to pack up and go to Cornwall or to Eckington where Robert has furnished a house in the village. He found the landlord had left a dozen or more little birds, budgerigars, in a cupboard and two gold fish in a pie-dish in the sink. He writes Bee that he wants bird-seed, the birds are so beautiful with such vivid colours; "don't bring any more supplies," he writes, "only bird-seed. I want to keep these birds alive."

I do not want to go to Cornwall or to Eckington, for that matter. It unnerves me to think of another move. The emotions of daily life, even living in one's own usual surroundings are so vivid, I can't stand any more. Sometimes, when one hears the wings (the buzz-zz-zz that is the Nazi, not "us") one almost thinks, if only now—now—if only it came quickly. Life is really not worth living, how can it be, how pretend it is?

It is pretty false to exaggerate. Yet almost, the only real thing now, is the buzz-zz-zz of the enemy wings overhead. We miss them if they don't come; stare at the ceiling and wonder, who is getting it now? If they rain fire and bombs on us, at least, they are here, we know where they are. This is perhaps an externalization of hidden inner terrors; a terror rationalized. It brings a sort of peace and the enemy now seem the only reality.

Perhaps they are the only reality.

We can't stand it any more. But we do stand it. This is what is interesting. When a man is dying, they say, his life flashes across; or if a man is dying, suffering, they say, sometimes he ceases to suffer and in the last agony, feels nothing. There is that. We reach the end, and if we can sustain sanity and detachment and discernment, we are each of us, in a singular and privileged position. We are each one of us a Galileo, a Newton. We may make discoveries that the human mind has not yet, so far, been in a position to make, about the human mind. If we can be the doctor, alive, watching ourself dying, we may come across some amazingly important and staggering discoveries. This sets a sort of fire burning. It is a blue fire, burning it is true, in a vacuum, but it is fire.

We have a blue-flame in our skull, rather like the blue-slide of my black-out lantern. There is a blue light, if you slide the little catch, on the electric torch, one way; there is the white or yellow light when you slide it in the opposite direction. It is like that. The white or yellow light is the ordinary light of human reason, the usual human mind-voltage. The blue light is for extra occasions; I switch on the blue when I go out in the black-out.

There are blue lamps everywhere. There must be these high-powered cerebral minds at work everywhere. Now, I feel quite alone, cut off; I write because the little blue flame in my skull, needs me in order to burn. I write just anything as just now, "I tangled myself in the cord of my reading-lamp" and then let the words run along. What are the words? I do not stop to consider them. I feel simply a click, as it were, and that other-mind is burning in my mind.

People write from America, "what are you writing? Won't you send your manuscripts to us here to keep for you? It would be interesting to see what you are writing," and I feel, but this is not writing. They will not understand that this is burning, that this is a flame in a skull, and that this flame must meet another flame, other flames, as the electric-torch picks out, in the damp and dank and murk of our London streets at night, the distant steady, strange little gleam of another distant electric torch, coming or going or crossing a street or climbing onto a bus. It is black, unutterably, the human consciousness. But maybe where it is most terribly dense, this blackness, there will be more opportunity for those lights to show.

I am thinking of those blue-lights, burning in skulls, burning out bodies that have become baffled with conditions of the simplest living. I am thinking of others who have said, we can't bear it but who go on, because of the immense adventure of going on where the human mind has not yet penetrated, making a path in the pitch-black night.

Tide-Line

(January 1941)

Now he takes my temperature, puts his hand on my wrist. "The trouble," he says, "is not a temperature but an under-temperature." I have probably been feeding my blue-brain (that part of my mind that does my living for me) too much. But he doesn't detract from the reality of that world, with his words. I am in both dimensions at the same time. (My desk-lamp is flickering and now I try the other lights and they all pulse and beat as if about to go out at any minute; some power-house in trouble.)

– – – – –

So the 4th dimensional world, the world of dream, of vision, of the blue-light, as I call it, high-powered thought, and the ordinary world come together. If I call the ordinary world, and its mental equivalent, the yellow light of the torch, then I suppose the intermediate world, the blue and the yellow together, should be green. It is perhaps the green world of rest, grass, trees, the level surface of the sea between tides. The full tide perhaps is the wash-up of externals; when the tide recedes, it leaves hidden beings and plants on that relatively infinitesimal strip of wet sand, that is ground common to both sea and land. When the tide of ordinary thought recedes, it can show these strange creatures, a phosphorescent jelly-fish, a star-fish, some trail of rare plant torn from a tropic sea-bed, a pebble of cornelian, coral-branch or amber. Those unusual treasures are the findings of the 4th dimensional mind, the inspirational mind or dream mind, but while we live in this world, we can not sustain that way of thinking, that way of vision for long. The tide of ordinary thought and living returns, covers the trail of exotic weed, erases the lovely print of shell, lifts the stranded jelly-fish back to its element. The high-powered image can not be sustained. It is drawn slowly back to the deep sea of universal thought. We must sadly watch it go, or more sadly watch it die, stranded above the tide-line.

Warehouse

(January 1941)

We wake in a black fog, it is later than it seems. I watch for the crack of dim light that should show between my curtain and the ceiling. But it is eight and pitch-black in my room. This is the morning that we are due to go out to Battersea, the other side of the river, to unearth a lot of old boxes where Bee has stored her mother's china and pictures. I have been dreading this. Bee says maybe the fog is too thick but we do get off soon after ten.

The city is desolate. We drive through mist, there are the usual gaps in our rows of houses, we notice them more in unfamiliar districts, we so soon grow accustomed to our own ruins. It is a ruinous sort of day altogether and I try my best to keep up some appearance of good humour. Can any thing more depressing be imagined than driving through war-London, to a warehouse in order to sift over a mid-Victorian past?

Notices at the gate, say "danger, no smoking," but Bee says it is the usual riverside peace-time precaution. We drive through the entrance to the yard and are shown into an enormous barn, piled high with boxes; a stray chintz-covered sofa is placed facing the enormous lift-shaft with its iron gates. We are to go up in that somewhere, or down. A key with a label is fastened to a nail in the wall, "for warden."

The manager at the entrance office has gone off to find the men in charge; a tired-looking apologetic individual at last appears, in brown overalls, with Bee's letter in his hand. He thought it was *next* Tuesday, not this that we were expected. He will however, himself lend a hand and get the boxes out and the contents in order. This is too much. Bee must not know that I am raging inwardly.

She says, will I wait in the car; "O no." "It's cold for you." But it is cold for her and she has that dreary little dry-cough. I wait beside the sofa, it must be damp; I feel if I sat down I would never get up again. There is the enormous iron cage of the lift and the steps down and the steps up. The workman has gone upstairs, so at least we will not be immured in the still damper cellar. He returns at last.

We go up several flights and there is a wilderness, a grand-piano, some kitchen chairs; another workman is helping. They arrange large gilt-framed pictures along the wall and against wooden crates and boxes. We are to select a bright one with sunlight in it for our friend, Dr. Walter's consulting room. At least, that is something. Picture after picture is dragged out, paper strews the floor; old newspapers were packed around the frames but here and there a glass is broken and broken glass adds to the general desolation.

The overhead light is not so bad, but I think, "this is the river-edge, opposite Chelsea," and though I don't usually care what happens in daylight, I think (in this twilight of despair) how filthy it would be to be caught in this tinder-box, with straw, old newspapers, and I realize that our whereabouts may not be known. If I go out unexpectedly, I place a notice on Bee's typewriter and she does the same to me. We must know where the other is and where the child is. But now, the girl is feverish, announces with a spot of swank, that she has the "new blitz-flue." Well, I might have told her where we would be. I did vaguely mention on the telephone last night, that we would be out all morning at the warehouse.

I think my ears must distantly have sensed the siren before realizing it entirely, for the sirens as if by pre-arrangement, arrived with this thought-alarm. The workmen took no notice whatever, and once the sirens had wheezed and whistled their full strength out, I felt better. Even the pictures looked different. "Why this is really so beautiful," I said to Bee. "Yes and this and this. Who is going to have this?" Then it seemed to me (so strangely) that I would like a huge old-fashioned, Victorian room, yes, go back to the mid-Victorians, be secure, be comfortable, know where I was, know where my friends were, no crazy, demented or dimensional way of thinking, a thick blue carpet (I could see the room) the walls not too crowded of course but this, this very thing with the thick-edged expensive elegant frame.

I held the picture up, it was one of the smaller ones. There it was. "Taormina?" I asked Bee. It was probably Sicily as they had often gone there and I remembered how Bee's mother had liked to talk to me about Egypt and Italy, especially Sicily.

Then it seemed to me supremely important that the pictures should not be lost, that sometime, I should see them all again. Not such very good pictures, Salon with their numbers, not Louvre or National Gallery but pleasant pictures, such as we might have had at our own art exhibitions when I was a girl. It was that level, pre-modern, nice thick blobs of ordinary paint, or post-Impressionist paint, yet preserving a picture-book reality. "But this is Capri."

The frames are heavy, the pictures lie stacked in rows, like pictures waiting to be hung, rather than taken down, packed away, discarded. We are really selecting some pictures as "jokes" for Robert who is furnishing his country house with relics of his own mother's furniture. This is the house where the bird-seed is wanted, and now I think nothing could be pleasanter myself, than to have such a house.

We find a harem-belle dancing (in tulle) on a rug, the rug is red but not too red. The pictures have second-rate stamped all over them, but second-rate with first-rate taste. Or rather first-rate that could say, "I'll buy what I want, don't tell me what to buy," which was more or less Bee's father's attitude to the pictures he collected. "This is Sicily, this is Capri, this—but this is Saint Mark's" I say. "Yes, it is Saint Mark's," says Bee, "you better have it." "Where could I possibly put it," but yes, a sense of property suddenly overwhelms me, yes, yes, I must have this Saint Mark's, it isn't a painted photograph, no, it is really a lovely delicate painting, and another in dimmer outline, less realistic is turned over by Bee, an interior, "and is this Saint Mark's, too?" she says.

I smell the incense. Incense has softened the stark outline of the pillars. Yes, I will have it too. But now Bee says it isn't Saint Mark's, she thinks it's a cathedral in Palermo. But it is the same mosaic, the same pillars, the same curves of age-old arches, like gold caverns under the sea. There is that sea-feeling in it, a temple under the sea.

"Who is having this?" I ask. "O, that better go to Cornwall with the others" she says. "I can leave them there, and get them back at any time." Yes, the people at St. Keverne must have the fishing scenes, the moors with violet streaks of heather, the village and the sea-scape. You'd think they would want to get away from sea-scapes, but that is what they are like, perched a half-mile from the sea.

But we must find some more "jokes" for Robert. "Will the harem-scene do?" "Yes, and this harlequin dancing; a sort of Mozart world, might be Russian ballet, he'd like it." We find some eminently funny ones, two donkeys, probably Sicilian, munching bright carrots and a blond of the Edwardian-French school. "He must have some good ones too, not just jokes, and will this do for Walter?" she says as we turn up a bright flower-stall backed by what must be French sunlit walls. She thinks that would please Dr. Walter and we find another French scene with houses along a stream, and a river with trees, really beautiful, for Robert.

The temples and the Capri and Sicilian scenes are placed with the lot for Cornwall, as Bee will save those for herself or give them to friends later. They won't go quite out of her hands and she asks where "my" pictures are to go, to Cornwall or Robert at Eckington.

I say "Eckington," as it is nearer. There are some of those grass-woven fancy palm-leaf fans, being flung out now with china. I'll take them, certainly no one else will want them. What do I want with six fans, worked with straw-pattern flowers? I once got some baskets like those in Capri. I don't think they would mean anything to anyone else. Now Bee says I must have the clock. It is shoved over with some difficulty, and I wade through straw and papers and broken glass. It is a lovely clock, there is an inlaid pattern of birds and a great gold minute-hand and a great fat hour-hand and a reasonable second-hand in a circle, about the size of a large watch. Will my house hold this ticking?

I said it would be difficult to house the clock, but certainly I will have the clock.

Everybody always had a clock like that, who had a house. It will take some time fortunately for the clock to be repaired, and delivered. Of course it may never be repaired and delivered. There may be—no—there is no use saying that, we take all that for granted. Perhaps that is why, in the dampness, standing in old newspapers, straw and broken glass, the clock released in me some spring of consciousness, some watch-spring or clock-spring. There *is* new-time, of course, to be established, but let us stick to our old time as well.

The Last Day

(January 1941)

The last day of the first month of the year, Jo and I have lunch together in the basement restaurant of the apartment store, next door. Streams of shop-assistants, girls and women and back-stage work-women in coarse aprons, make a stage-set or film-set of this small somewhat shabby Edwardian dining-room. As the all-clear goes, they all stream out again, from the shelter behind the restaurant. The all-clear is soon followed by another alarm or alert, as we say, and down they come again. This goes on; it gives an odd sense of unreality, as if these were really supers, called for duty in a crowd scene, dismissed, recalled.

We seem to be in another town, although my apartment is a stone's throw away. We seem to be in some provincial Leeds or Manchester; the people look different, they are my next-door neighbours during working hours. The things in the shop have a Hollywood appearance of slightly provincial Edwardian smartness. The details one feels are cleverly worked out. We ourselves are in and of this. It is like this all the time; we are all actors, all the time.

We go back to my rooms and Jo stays on for tea, the girl comes in. When the guns were quiet and a final all-clear went, they both slid off. It is dark and cold, not yet five, with thick mist. The gun-fire seemed to come through blankets or thud artificially from a distant "lot."

- - - - -

I was thinking of a dream I had a few nights ago, during my fever. The side of a room, my own room, seemed to have slid away, but this was not unpleasant. It was suggested no doubt, by the houses we see, with rooms open to the street like stage-rooms, some are neatly sliced off with furniture still standing. So in my dream, the side of my room is sliced off. I am there with a pleasant intermediate crowd, undefined old friends.

This open-to-the-street room is dim, but now snow swirls and drifts and to my surprise as the snow whirls into the room, in a soft living cloud, I realize that the snow is not cold. It has all the qualities of snow, the whiteness, the lightness, the softness, the beauty—but this snow is as natural as air, it fills the room as air made visible.

Through the rifts there are stars; one great cluster seems almost artificial, picked out in rose, yet it is natural and mysterious as any star-cluster. I do not remember the name of the constellation or even if in the dream I identified it, but I feel the name of the special cluster or constellation would hold some key or clue. However the great cluster vanishes and we are looking into the normal, distant powder-dust of small stars. Then I seem to say to myself that the stars really had manifested in snow-form, that the dust of stars and the snow are the same.

It is a dream of peace and hope. It seems to indicate that though our houses and our minds have been sliced open by the attacks of the enemy overhead, that, overhead is as well, the great drift of stars, and those stars found entrance into the shattered house of life.

Nefert

(April 1941)

My lovely little cat Nefert, whom I had in Switzerland, when I lived there with my mother during the last years of her life, was gathered to the shades, some decade and a half ago, or even twenty years ago. Shades? The familiar siren wails, just as I am comfortably in bed. It is a horrible reminder and never fails in its effect. Simply, the mind asks, is this my last night on earth? Life did not seem so splendid in the lotus-years after the last war, those "lost" years as many of the last war generation, have come to call them. But now life has a new occultation, a new phase; we want (through curiosity, through some new-sensed will-to-live) to see around the corner; having endured, more than a hundred violent raid-nights, (roughly three hundred raids in all, they tell us, up to date) we want some reward, I suppose for this endurance. We don't want to die to-night. Not this way, not in the uncertainties, questioning, will I be burnt to death? will I suffocate? will I fall through my own floor? will my own wall fall on me? We ask ourselves these questions, we don't dodge these possibilities. This way madness lies or does not lie. The nightmare is outside.

– – – – –

Nefert is an Egyptian word and means beautiful. So beauty manifested in my dream in the form of my little cat, not much more than a kitten. She is prowling about Bee's room and I wrap her in a bright figured handkerchief, that I had bought in Vienna, many years ago. I put her in a bag a friend brought me from a cruise, and take her into the front room, where I leave her under the piano, while I go out to the kitchen to get her milk. I shake her out of the bag and am horrified and alarmed to find that during my very short absence, she has had kittens. Two perfectly marked tiny Siamese kittens sit on the Vienna handkerchief, they have the perfect black martin mask of the mother; this is frantically upsetting, somehow. I am terribly distressed to think of my little cat having had these kittens.

This upsets me so much. Bee and the brilliantly intellectual Elfrida come in. I try to communicate to them my feeling and they are kind but only vaguely interested. They seem more interested in a card-game they are about to play. A game! I suppose, in my dream, I am feeling that there is a gap in consciousness, they are both brilliant and active, but I feel (I must feel, in my dream) inferior, in some way. The backs of the cards have a pattern of gallants in an old-fashioned garden. I seem to want to make doubly sure that this is a game, that their life, (which actually I admire and envy) is indicated on the back of the playing cards as well by the cards themselves. I seem to want to stress the fact that all this brilliance that I so admire and this success, is a game. They are playing a game with cards that have a scene of light-hearted amusement on their backs. They do not seem unsympathetic but I know they do not realize what a shock this has been, my little cat has had kittens.

She Is Dead

(June 1941)

I run after her. I do not know who she is. She is dead. Like a child running through a familiar street, I run in the dusk, in the dark. Someone, vaguely familiar, yet unidentified seems to help drag along this sledge-like cart or carriage. Maybe there is a companion, but my concern is chiefly to keep up with this, I must not lose sight of the sledge-drawn cart. The white veiled shape is conventional, like a snow-lady a child fashions, a statue. Yet it is a person, it is someone; who is it? I do not know who it is. Snow-white might be her name; this might be a street from a picture-book, it is dark, I do not identify the houses, we must hurry. Secretive, too, we must be secretive, there is something to be lost, we must not lose this. This snow-lady, this dead-lady belongs to us, to myself and the self-double who drags or draws the sledge.

Waking in a room that has been insufferable with this sudden London June heat-wave, I stare into the darkness. The cold is translated as night wind through the curtains. I wonder who that was? Myself? Is it myself? Have I really at last died or has that part of me which was dead and frozen been at last projected, symbol of life and death? Is this an infantile death-wish, residue of child death-wish? Is this some friend? Is this the whole era, the whole age? Is this a symbol of the past? Who is this lady? Yes, it is part of myself, I conclude, that has died, but now it is projected out. Maybe, after all, I will survive this war. It seems to me that I am more alive than I have been for many years. That must have been myself. A dream of a funeral, according to the old adage, means, by contrast, joy, or crudely translated, a wedding. Am I to come back to life, to be wed to life after all?

— — — — —

I am sustained through the day. It is a new day. It is June 20, 1941, almost Midsummer day. I have only to think "she is dead, she is dead" and a wave of joy and hope sustains me. I have carried her with me, I think, almost my whole life. She was a stalactite-self, she was neatly fitted in myself, it seems, her coffin. She was wrapped in the layers of my growing self, like a nun in her enveloping garments. Only sometimes she looked out of my eyes, she passed over my face, her mouth was my mouth, the mobile mask of my outer face was replaced by her static frozen mask. Then people drew back. O, I have frightened people or she has frightened them. She was wise, she was not so much arrogant in her wisdom, as lost. She had only this peculiar garment of my own body to live in. It must have been a burden to her. There were very few occasions when she could express herself, sometimes I wrote for her, stalactite-shaped running verse that, on a page, looked broken, a stalactite with the ridges and furrows, frozen.

I am free of her, she is dead. She died the night of June 20, 1941, I think after mid-night, yes, surely it must have been just before dawn.

Saint Anthony

There needn't be anything. What there was was the large flat square table. On the table there was practically nothing although he was a very busy man.

His secretary had taken his own chair and he was sitting on the low couch that was drawn up along the opposite side and her back was half turned toward me as I came in the door and she did not swivel round in the chair but she kept on writing. She was taking notes in a note-book. She was holding the note-book, it was not flat on the table and he went on talking.

I crossed the room. That is Anthony Eden, I thought. I thought, I would not disturb them and I really was surprised when he got up and followed me across the room. The secretary seemed to go on writing with her back half turned. He bent to kiss me so that he was taller than I thought or I was smaller. I was smaller. I was not a child but I was grown-up enough to be frightened when he tugged at my dress and said, come over to the couch. No, no, no, I said. I was not elated nor really frightened and my dress was very pretty. That is, it was a perfect dress, I did not notice it at all, except to think afterwards, why that was a perfect dress, I did not notice it at all.

The dress fell to the floor, there was no feeling of a collar, it was what we used to call an afternoon dress, I suppose, or it was a summer dress in the days when we wore summer dresses. It was a real dress and it had a colour, but it was not green nor yellow. I did not wear a hat and my hair was light brown, not gold, not brown, it was not long nor short, it was tucked around in such a way that you would never think of its falling down but it was up rather than down. Of course, my dress was not red or blue; I mean when I say it was not green, not yellow that it was that sort of intermediate colour of leaves that leaves have when certain birch or beech leaves are uncurled and out but not quite flat; they are a little crinkled and gold-brown or rather green-gold where they will be green. That is the way with the dress too, it was not crinkled but there was that feeling. I had come out with it on. That is, it showed what sort of thing I was, what sort of tree I belonged to, what family perhaps of tree, because I can not think of myself thinking in that large empty room of having any family. Anthony Eden was not my family, his secretary was not my mother.

$-\ -\ -\ -\ -$

What I thought was, this is a saint and I was very happy. I knew of course that it was not Anthony Eden but I knew that it was Anthony and I knew that it was Eden. He was dark, Spanish or Portuguese (the later Anthony) or burnt with the desert, that other Anthony the Hermit. He was a saint in modern dress of course, for that is how a saint would be.

By a very obvious series of associations he was Secretary of State for Foreign Affairs, he was Anthony, he was Eden, he was an important person. The State was not this British Commonwealth or any State of that sort but some sort of state of mind or spirit, and he was importantly associated with Foreign Affairs. He was not in that sense English nor was he in that sense American but his great wide room with the bright dim light suggested one of those fabulous elaborately simple rooms you see on the films, generally filled with a crowd of Wall-Street potentates or diplomats. He was associated with foreign things and he was foreign but for me he manifested himself as of to-day, as of this city in which I live, or one of its companion cities of America or even of South America.

The light seemed to indicate sunlight outside and though there were no windows, there was yet the inference that if there had been windows, there would have been no sort of curtain or black-out curtain. The light filtered evenly into the room and there were no apparent shadows. This of course I sensed, my whole being was absorbing the room and its peculiar characteristics, its beauty of line, its length, its light, its unbroken wall and long floor and the way the door had opened.

I did not float at all into the door, I opened the door although I do not think I turned a handle and I did not knock. It was the answer to *knock and it shall be opened unto you*, but I had done the knocking before I went to sleep but I had not actually named Anthony or maybe I had. I had a string of beads that a friend had given me, they were actually a rosary but the rosary I believe, originated in Tibet so my rosary given me by this friend—who was, if anything, a Buddhist by conviction—yet allowed my mind to make this compromise, my heart could play over the beads and I did not think any more, because I was middle-aged and tired of thinking.

My mind had been shattered and I had tried various ways and means of healing-thought and of expression and now at the last, I just "played" my beads at night before I went to sleep. If I named a saint it was as legendary a personality as any wizard or good fairy out of folk-lore, yet I had named Anthony, naming a person for every bead. Anyhow, I had named Anthony and I had lighted tapers for him in the *Kapuzinerkirche* some years before, in Vienna while Vienna yet was.

– – – – –

I lighted the tapers before the dingy shrine of Saint Anthony because the church was dark and it was cold and there was a cluster of beggars seated along the bench against the wall. They looked around when the flap before the inner door lifted or when there were footsteps in the outer corridor.

They had crept in for shelter, stealing a little rest on the benches and I had crept in out of curiosity and because an open church door always compels me to enter. There were bones, as I remember, under glass and a general air of rococo grandeur in decay. I knew that downstairs in the crypt, there were some mummies with imperial regalia but I did not feel that I could face them that day; it was *Kapuzinerkirche*, church of the Capuchin, there was a statue of a monk in the Franciscan habit in the niche over the round window.

The round window was cut in the white plaster of the outer-wall as if a cookie-tin had cut its circle in white rolled dough and there were the two oval side-windows exactly symmetrical, either side of the projecting outer porch or vestibule. That had its round circular topped door and the two smaller side doors with a small round window over each. There was a small cross over the door and a larger cross on top of the church, set in a ring like a weather-vane and there was the steeple with very narrow shuttered windows and its plain cross on the roof-cone.

It was exactly a church a child might copy from a drawing-card or drawing-book and I had copied it many times for I knew this church and I could even put in the slight symmetrical trimmings under the peak of the roof and over the door.

The fanlight over the door had six sticks if you count the upper level of the door as two.

That was outside the church, you saw this as you crossed the square or *platz*, whose name I can't remember. I remember the faces of the beggars as they peered furtively around as I pushed up the worn leather flap. Were they afraid of being turned out? I walked around and came back to the beggars.

There were a few candles and I thought, I am a heretic and this is a sort of stealing but if I light the candles before the shrine of Saint Anthony, I am lighting them for the beggars because it will make the corner here a little brighter and because after all I am a baptized Christian. I even dropped to my knees on the cold stone as I saw the beggars turn from the sight of the peculiarly devout lady who was lighting all the candles. The beggars bowed their heads and I (just in time) dropped to the stone floor, as a replica of the carved Franciscan over the door outside, entered from somewhere behind the altar. We were all praying like mad as his beads rattled past us and out of the door.

The Ghost

(Spring 1941)

The Venetian mirror was, she thought, put together in two pieces; they were of one period and the glass was flawed. The frame was silver-grey. The surface of the old glass was grey-green. It was or was not one of the outstanding treasures of the room, she stood in.

Her back was to the window. Outside she felt the cool, translucent green of young-spring branches. The man who stood behind her loomed disproportionate. She felt his presence, she knew he was there, but his being there was as impersonal as the wave of cold green that would be, she believed, reflected in the old glass, if she moved slightly to the right. As she stood, she saw nothing in the mirror.

Then it occurred to her in the bright daylight, that if she moved forward or moved a half-pace to the right, placed herself directly before the frame, she would perhaps see nothing at all. It occurred to her that this might be, to use the new phrase they had coined, a "booby-trap."

Or you would look in the mirror and there would be your face, your contour, the blue voile of the shaped turban, the slightly worn nap of the blue cloth jacket, the soft woven-wool pattern of the Persian design of the scarf, knotted at your throat. The face would be angular, with the lines and planes refined down, not so much distorted as conventionalized and depersonalized by fatigue. You would see that face, recognize it and at the gentle persistence of the mannered voice going on and on, as if frightened not so much for himself as for you, you would frown slightly at the reflection, with the glass flaws lending plausibility to the reflection—for that dot-dot-dot like a ripple on static grey-green of the clouded lagoon, would stand between you, facing the mirror and the slightly unfamiliar reflection.

Like Euclid, you could step forward and by drawing a mental straight line, you could prove angles, an angle of incidence (was it?) that correlated or equaled, an angle of reflection? Then having proved that a dot-dot-dot was a flaw in seventeenth century, miraculously unbroken glass, and made, as it were, a perfect little fence or hedge between self and reflected self, and that there was a self standing on a square of carpet and a self in the natural order of things, reflected, at its proper distance, you could answer the voice, play the game that it was so anxiously playing. He thinks I am quite mad. He does not however, know it.

If I step forward and look straight into the glass and there is no reflection, I will have to tell him. He will be kind about that. He will say, "yes, yes, I wondered if it would work that way. I think that last occasion that it mani-fested was in my grandfather's time, about 1860, May it was, just this time of the year. As a matter of fact, do you mind stepping over those portfolios, I brought you here particularly to show you this set of Chinese paintings; I don't know that the frame for that second one, the violin or zither with the melon, goes as well with the slightly stripey parchment colour, as the unvar-nished oak of the one hanging—or didn't you notice it—to the left of the dolphin-table you so admired, at the turn of the stairs."

He would say something like that, but there would be more of it, more carefully and particularly, yet very quickly pronounced, with several careful dates, "would it be, do you think 1780 or the second empire"—but that was the little dancing figures, that repeated themselves in porcelain on a circle of glass on the dining-room table, around the heap of striped rose and white ca-mellias. When she had spoken of the flowers, at lunch-time, he had said, "yes, yes, they recall some specially artificial period, don't you think, I can't decide whether it's 1780 or the second empire."

— — — — —

She would see the face, angular, and not so much chizzeled as worn away, whittled away or gnawed into by fatigue. Or not. She would see a skull; that stone skull, crowned with heavy raw un-cut priceless jewels in the Hradčany on the hill in Prague, was the one of which she now thought, standing on the strip of carpet before the Venetian glass that was not broken but fitted in two sections; the lower one was about a third or a quarter the width of the upper.

The glass was evidently fitted like that, the two pieces matched. There was the clear dark line, drawn like an ink-line on a piece of slightly tinny sil-ver paper. This separated the upper section of the old glass from the lower. But for almost an infinitesimal segment of a second, as she stood on the carpet and heard the voice going on, she knew that the black line would dissolve, that she would stand there and turn and answer the voice or that she would step slightly to the right and face the glass; she would face the glass and she would or she would not see the direct reflection, through the long narrow window at her back, of the meticulously outlined branches of the beech-trees. The leaves would be reflected ridiculously and meticulously in the flawed silver of the Venetian mirror. They were drawn, each leaf separate with ridiculous painstaking care; the colour, criticising, you would say, was ridiculous; there was too much gold in the young green, the leaves were too perfect, the trunks of the tall trees were too amber and the spring shadows that May morning—for it was still morning by the sun—too insistently differentiated.

The sweep of the drive was ordinary, there were country cows, not long horned elk in the grass. Behind the house, there were sheds and pig-pens and a walled garden that any child might pencil carefully, with a well and a bucket, from a copy in a drawing-book. Carefully, any thoughtful child might draw the house, the steps, the crenulated turrets of the roof, the separate squares of the stone building-blocks. Carefully, any child might, almost you might say set up the house, the Hall, from stone-bricks; carefully, he might pencil it, in a drawing-book from this obvious original. Carefully—O, nothing of these words formed any thought in her head, as she stood on the square of carpet. But careful, something whispered; though she was acquainted with the voice, it came from a cavity. It came from a vacuum, it came from nowhere.

She did not step to the right, she did not test the mirror. She did not test herself; it was all a charade, a masque here. Here, it was more than a game of keeping one's head up, it was more than a trial of unrecorded endurance. There was no note-book, no text-book, no religious manual, no prayer-book to show them here how to direct knees, how to conduct hands, how to correlate elbows. The whole skeleton had come alive, a skeleton in a cupboard; everyone in London had it.

A curious thing, a mechanical and so far dependable instrument was in the top part of the skeleton; that round ball or box was like the pine-cone set upon the rod of the god. It was set there, a head, a brain, for the receiving and the recording of sound, of thought, of vision. That was what the round pine-apple or pine-cone of the head, was meant for. But it had been devoted for the last year or year and a half, to quite another function. It directed, within a body, a set of bones, it jerked a wrist upward or directed extremely clever knee-joints and ankles to perform cleverly the act of walking. It opened lips, cleverly so that you did not hear the wooden clatter of the lips when talking, of the Ventriloquist's dummy that you were. The thing talked. You heard it talking. You forgot to be astonished any more, at its ingenuity.

– – – – –

It was important that this doll, this dummy, this recording instrument that received, through delicate sets of receiving stations, wave-lengths of sound, vibrations of light, should not be broken. Ironically she thought, or perceived through that medium for which we have few descriptive phrases or even defining names, that if only for the recording of the sound of the voice, speaking as it were off-stage, though in reality projecting its tones and half-tones a few feet behind her shoulder in that small room, it would be a pity if it were lost. It had endured fifty odd years, a half century and it was not yet worn out.

Oddly it was only just now, she felt tuned or toned or weathered or seasoned like a violin. She could record a whisper or a breath, could differentiate good or bad, kindness or indifference, intolerance or mere casual acceptance. She was there for recording—who was it had once called her a Recording Angel?

Indifferent, tired to death, she knew the ultimate indifference. It was there in that glass. What she saw, would see, might blaze such a heady trail of realization that even she might be blinded by it. That sort of blinding could cauterize her brain. It would be a flash, a white-hot searing iron and then no more, not ever any more, pain. It was something she had earned, as she had on several other separate occasions, earned the right to escape. She had this time, not died once in London, but fifty times at least, as many times put it, as she had years to the mere calendar record of her life. Say one death for one year and the other two or three casual deaths that had happened before this particular epoch of war-years, could be discounted as little experiments in dying.

Say she had been burnt to death in the last year, and smothered and broken by falling masonry; once or twice, she might have been smashed on a pavement while leaping from the lap of flames across her own carpet; once or twice, she might have died miserably half-conscious in a shelter with the bombs still falling outside. Of being crippled for life, she had no fear. Someone had told her that someone-in-the-know had told *her*, that they were going mercifully to "put out" more or less hopeless cases; they would not have room nor time for cozening the living-dead. That was a comfort; no mattress grave, at any rate.

Jaunty and pert, she stood on the square of carpet now, in the very-private writing-room of this well-known much publicized critic, poet and novelist. Much photographed, much caricatured, there was the ridiculous proud head that, in the years immediately following the last "great" war, she had been wont to find pompous, self-inflated, frivolous, flippant, self-conscious and superficial. It had hounded you from the illustrated papers, you came to associate that Roman profile with the dentists, the hair-dresser, for those were the only occasions, while waiting, that you deigned to leaf over this type of fashionable journal. It put her out, somehow, that suave, breezy success. She knew actually that this sort of publicity meant almost life and death to this aristocrat, this poet. He needed the money, they said. He was land-poor and treasure-poor, for his treasures (they were all around her in this house) could not, she believed, be sold, not that he would ever sell them. But even had he wanted to sell them, many of them were not his, to sell. They belonged to the nation and the nation was England and the nation, which she had so loved from the beginning, was poor.

– – – – –

The new post-war generation was on the way. It was waiting, outside that window, to crowd them off the scene. They were escapists, they lived in the much-maligned ivory-tower. They had no sense of the "realities," the new voices protested from Arizona and New Mexico, from the Pacific Coast, or from the hide-away of their Pacific coast in England. There was one answer to that, she had it. How many blitz-nights, did you spend in London? This was poor pride.

The effects, it was scientifically stated, of war-shock were not at once, registered. You stiffened, you endured, you waited for the next bout of bombing. Were bombs reality? If so, were the realists, who theorized about the new Britain, the new England, the new World, in the thick of it? Whose fault was it? And if yours and theirs, in what way would they, would you, record it?

Temperamentally, she herself could now at this moment draw as if it were a film across her eyes; the flawed glass would become a diviner's crystal. Was that reality? Was what went on here, these ghosts in this house, tangible presences, real? If so, she was one of the realities. Did they know, the realists, the reality of the ghost-world? Shelley was real. Proust whom they now anathematized was real. The late Mrs. Woolf who walked into a river, but a few weeks ago, was real. She was real. Her death was a sign of failure, or not? Having done her work, one camp protested, she was well out of it. Had she done her work?

What was her work? What was the work of the artist? One of them, the most sensational manifestation of the last post-war generation stood at her shoulder; he would keep out the unreality (would he?) of the new Britain. What was the new Britain? What would become of this house? What would become of the twisted angular beauty, that lady Elfrida, his sister who at this moment was seated in the yellow-brocade chair before the fire in the room she and her brother had just, some five or some ten minutes ago, left?

In five, in ten minutes he had whirled her through the hall into several bed-rooms, his work-room, to show her some rare prints. In her head was the swift succession of impressions, birds framed in dark narrow wood, a bedspread with a rose-shell design of Cupids, butterflies, Psyche, sea-shells, the long mirror in his own (she surmised) bed-room with the carved shells or the real shells arranged and fastened to the mirror frame and gilded. She had wanted to ask him if they were carved shells or real shells gilded, but he had whirled her about in that short time, in that short space, "this dancing group was painted by an old Harlequin, don't you like the living quality of the figures, you see being actually a dancer" . . . he named a French name that left no memory of words but the chime of French, the French syllables like a tune, ran a run of notes in the easy flow of his own prose that he always uttered.

There was a window looking out over the sunken-garden and a topiary tree, and slightly shabby (even from this height) squares of box, around empty garden beds. The statues he said, had been wrapped up all winter. This he said (talking by the window) was a special day, a sort of fête-day for him, it always was, the first spring day when the statues were unwrapped. What are they wrapped in, she asked, simply for the sake of making a dialogue of this engaging monologue and he said (if she remembered) that they were wrapped in old sacking and (did he say?) dried leaves. She would never know just what he said, for the recording instrument, the mind, no matter how carefully adjusted, does not retain more than the tiniest fraction of the received impression. And though she could say, standing in her blue voile turban cap, her dark blue skirt and jacket, that wrappings had dropped, dead leaves and sacking of false thought, exaggerated and wrong ways of thinking had peeled off or dropped off, she could not say just when and where that had happened. Decorous at least, at least it's all right. At least Elfrida, the frightening and fabulously intellectual beauty, had smiled at her across the table.

At least, even if she had babbled and burbled and screamed and flung herself or been flung into an epileptic fit (some sign of release from that nightmare of London) they would have known how to deal with her. At least, she hadn't talked too much, she had talked, she had followed every gesture of the butler and her hand had not trembled when she scooped out the slippery dressed salad leaves into the crescent-shaped or half-moon plate that was, she had realized in a panic, shoved away the other side of the bread and butter plate, too far to be dealt with properly. But she had successfully conveyed slippery leaves to a half-moon salad plate that was not, as she had expected easily at her elbow.

A clock had struck two, very slowly and the salad leaves had not slipped and slithered from the broad awkward spoons. The clock had lied, as so much, so much about her, in the dead leaves and sacking part of her, had lied. The clock had struck two slowly, and it was by the sun, two hours ahead of the real time. It was only a week since the new hour had been added to the one extra hour of summer-time that they had retained all winter, from last summer.

So, clocks, the infallible, were lying to them. Time and space were the same thing, accordion-pleated sensations could be folded close together, then by some miracle, time and space could be unfolded, and give out a tune. Time and space here played a tune and expectant of tricks, *poltergeist* manifestation even in broad daylight, she had not been expecting any personal miracle of readjustment. Really, it did not matter. Not any way. 1941, by an easy trick, could be resolved to 1914. Then all those post-war years of Lethe or stagnation, did not matter.

1941 or 1914 or, if you begin juggling with the figures, 1419 or 1491 made really the same pattern. A small vine-leaf, an out-size pâquerette, a large violet curved earthward; the numbers could resolve themselves, the curved head of the budded 9 could be plucked from the pattern—what were numbers? As long ago, as 1914, whispers were getting about, there was a German, there was a Jew, there was, by 1919 a tea-table topic, there was time and space, there was Einstein, there was relativity.

There was a German, there was a Jew. There have been too many Germans, there have been one or two, too many Jews; 1941 drew itself up; it was protected, either end, by the tall guardsman, the 1 and the 1 protected it at either end, it was fenced in, it was not left like 1914 with that 4, the cross, to be taken up, to be carried through the trail of the years. It was to have been all right afterwards.

What was afterwards? 1918, but that volitable 8 could be turned about; it was a pair of glasses; it was a cat, you could point ears and whiskers with a pencil; it was simply nothing and nothing, o and o, piled one upon the other. It was a spiral, you were caught in it, going round and round like a squirrel in a cage. But 1919 opened the door again, you ran out like quicksilver from a broken thermometer (that scale of time and hot and cold, was broken). You were out again, you were scattered like seed from a broken seed-pod. You were to be sown, like the parable seed, on good ground. You fell—on what? 1920 caught you back into the circle of eternity. You were caught again in the o, the eternal circle. Now indeed you were to be born, re-born. 1920 witnessed a strange metamorphosis.

— — — — —

The mirror that she faced, didn't cloud over. If it had, even at that, she could have brushed it aside, an optical delusion, I have been so tired. Her lungs seemed to be expanding with the young-green of the vibrant trees outside, and if she stepped to one side, no doubt, she would simply see the reflected long window at her back. He would be interested, however. At lunch time, she had been caught glancing up at the array of pictures like pictures in a famous gallery (they were pictures in a famous gallery). She had said, as he caught her glance, turned impolitely away from that little group about the table, "I like the pink youth."

There was her host at her side, her friend who had brought her here, was opposite. Criss-cross, beyond the oasis of pink and white camellias, was the famous face of the lady, Elfrida. They were talking of the things they talked about, a duck on a pond, "and I said, 'look at it,' he said, 'isn't it wonderful,' I meant, that it was like a duck on a screen-painting in the mist against the reeds, but he said, 'O, I was thinking how good it would be to eat'" . . . saying, "famine must have had an effect, don't you think, on the actual aesthetic ideas of nations, was it the memory of the siege of Paris—1870, I mean—that turned the minds of the French to food, made gourmets of them?"

She had listened to all this, but her eyes were drawn upward, where painted velvet caught the colour but not the texture of the flowers in the table-centre. Then the lady Elfrida's brother who seemed to feel her slightest gesture, followed her glance and as she came back quickly with the remark, "I like the pink youth," he had said, "yes," as if pleased at her choice of portraits, "that is the ghost."

Before the Battle

(London, Summer 1940)

So things rush over us suddenly. We go along, day by day, then an inevitable moment arrives, unexpectedly, when the Battle of Britain becomes something that actually may happen, and we stand shoulder to shoulder, living bodies, like the bodies that make up coral-islands, to contribute, to sacrifice our very bones to keep back the invader. But until we are sacrificed or sanctified by a new peace, inevitable waves of terror sweep over us, cosmic tide-waves of terror drown us. Many of us are familiar with a sort of rhythm of terror, like rhythm of birth-pangs, actually we are in travail, actually and literally in the sense of the Book of Revelations, we ourselves are begetting this new age.

In the grasp of blackness, she tried to get out of her mind her chief concern, Russia. The Russian news did not seem too good last night. If Russia should be against us? If Russia? It was an illogical fear, but this fear seizes us from time to time. Russia. Then she began to worry again about her child's book, about the future of her child, technically no longer a child, and the many children.

When she had exhausted herself in a sort of black-sweat of agony, she lay down on her couch. It was soon after ten. Then *the Lord is my shepherd*, she repeated over and over to herself. It answered better than the prayer she started. The Latin *Sancta Dei Genitrix, ora pro nobis*, acts like a charm sometimes, it dispels fear and opens doors. But the old call of the old-English, the rugged, rock-like beauty of the English version of the Psalm, was more suited to her mood. *I shall not want. He maketh me to lie down. Yea, though I walk through the valley of the shadow of death*, where we now walk.

But the door-bell sounded and she thought it must be an air-warden or a telegram from the Continent, where her friend is caught in Switzerland. But it was the child, she was worrying about. The child's book, she had decided, was the child herself, she feared misconstruction and misapprehension and actual criticism might be let loose by the publication of her child's autobiography, she feared that she herself would die. Struggling with this terror, she tried to face the fact that she had feared to die herself in 1919, when the child was born. Struggling with the remembrance of personal agony and threat of immediate death, which at the time nature (for the sake of life) had forced her to repress, she had sweated, as I say, in a sort of black agony. Then, she had spoken those words, *Yea though I walk through the valley. . . . I shall fear no evil. For thou art with me.* And the door-bell rang.

It was this same child who rarely came in, unless by prearrangement, at this time of night. She seemed a dream of beauty, in her summer frock. The pretty dress was printed with red flowers, like poppies and with green leaves. Around the child's thick soft dark hair, was a ribbon of a peculiarly tender shade of blue. The blue of the ribbon caught up blue flowers woven among the poppies and the green leaves of the summer print-frock she wore; hatless, stockingless in soft open suede slipper-sandals, the creature (modern, as she thinks, in the extreme) was yet tenderly and exquisitely (with no self-consciousness) attired like very Primavera. She was life. *He maketh me to lie down in green pastures.* Here was this pasture, a summer-field scattered with summer flowers.

– – – – –

"O come in, darling."

There she is, the daughter, standing in the hall. The child has stepped out of the door of life.

This is the short cut. God answers so subtly. So beautifully. I could not have thought of a lovelier thing in answer to my own prayer, why, she walked in unexpectedly, right on my words, *For thou art with me.* "Come in."

"But you've gone to bed. It's late."

"No but wait. I didn't draw the curtains, it's past black-out time." She shut her own door. She goes to the front room, to the side-room where she has her desk and does her writing, to the bath-room, to the little kitchen, groping in the dark, fastening the black-out curtains. Now the child switches on the overhead light in the big room. "No, put that out, let's have the other light." It is a wall bracket, glass, with a rose-coloured bulb shining out to shape the cut pattern of sun-shapes carved on the glass. The rose light falls on the child seated on the couch now, with the background of the fawn-coloured panel tacked up behind the cushions. She is a portrait, she is painted in bright summer-colours, her face is round and rose-coloured, her face is a red rose certainly. *O, my love is like a red, red rose.* Her grandmother was born in June and loved roses, this child was born with the spring sun rising and her other sign is Leo, she was born in the house of the beginning, the Ram with Leo, the house of pleasure rising. Pleasure? This is what had worried her mother in the book, the last part of the book. Parties.

"O—what happened at the party?"

"O, that was this afternoon, I met Jack there. He took me out to dinner last time, so I asked him out this. But you were asleep?"

"No, I couldn't read any more and I listened to the radio and then I was just drifting about, getting ready for bed, it's early."

"He was so cross about my book. He said I was selfish. He said the book was just about myself. He said, why did I write such a book at such a time with such terrible things happening."

"But the book is called *Pre-war*, it's about things that happened before the war."

"He said it was a selfish book, about myself, that I was selfish. He said, why did I have friends like that—that I didn't really care for my friends. That if one of them was shot in the . . . in the . . . I wouldn't care for him any more, that I wouldn't marry one of them, why did I go about with them, like that, when I wouldn't marry one of them?"

"Why should you marry one of them?"

"He kept saying it across the table. It was horrible. Why should he say it? He said, why do you have friends like that, when I said something half in joke about my men friends. He said, you say men, don't consider *me* in that light, just a man-friend. Why do you talk like that? Why do you say, men-friends like that? Get up, go away, there is the ladies entrance."

"What did he mean by there is the ladies entrance?"

"I don't know. I got up to go, then he came with me, and said, I'll get you a taxi, but there was no taxi and by the time a taxi came in sight, a bus came so I got on the bus. Then the bus stopped at the corner and I got off." ("At the exact moment when I started saying to myself *the Lord is my Shepherd*," she thought.)

"Then I came along, then I thought I'd come in, though it's late."

"What made you exactly come in—I mean you know it's lovely, once before, you came late after a party, I love you to come in, but why did you think of coming in?"

"O, the bus stopped at the corner and I thought I'd get out. I just thought I'd come in. Maybe you didn't want me?"

"O—yes—let me get you some fruit-juice." (She keeps a special pink-raspberry sort of thing, as the child remembers it from little circus treats and fairs and outings in Switzerland, but she doesn't realise why her mother keeps just that special raspberry or loganberry fruit-extract for her.) "I have some new grape-fruit juice, it's good with soda—have a cigarette?"

"No, I was smoking. No, I just had my dinner. Why did he say that about my book?"

"I don't know, darling. It's probably something purely pathological. You must remember that a book implies all sorts of things. We know how clever Jack is, how really successful, but he never had the big novel published that he was so keen about. He probably, in spite of all his clever articles, really wants to have a proper-sized book published. He mixed up the idea of a book with the idea of a baby, probably. He is a darling, you know, but rather twisted."

"He said, he had had more happen to him when he was twenty. Why didn't I do anything, have anything really happen in the book? He said it was all about myself."

"Well, books are in one way and another, all about the people who write them."

"He was quite nice at Dick's party."

"Who was at the party?"

"O Miss Janel, the novelist and Dick's cousin—"

"Yes, such a nice girl. I met her you know, at your birthday-party, sitting on the gramophone table, wasn't she, in the corner?"

"He and Pat got on. Then he said, why does Pat dislike me so much?"

"He was tight, I expect—you know he drops a stitch when he's tight sometimes."

"He went on about Pat."

"Or it's more like a landslide, one can listen for five hours, very tired and he never notices and he never gets anywhere."

"But he's nice the next day, he'll be nice when I see him at the Centre, in the morning."

"Well, then forget all about it. I say, it's this way. Men, the nice sensitive men, the unobvious ones, the sort we know for the most part, are creative and really they would like a child, not a child as a man has a child, but a child actually. So they get jealous when something like a child, a book, comes to a woman who can have a child anyway. They don't know they're like that, but that's why so many of them hate things women do. Because a woman is biologically so much more highly evolved than a man, then they think, why should a girl have everything? He is jealous of your book probably."

"But you're sleepy."

"No, darling. Now have a cigarette. You don't seem tight yourself." (This is how one talks to them).

"No. I just had sherry. Dick mixed some strong things the way he does but I don't have them usually."

"Who else was there?"

"O—you know, the sort of airmen that come in."

"O—yes. The sort of airmen who come in."

- - - - -

"Thank you for the hour," she said. She meant it. She might have been progressing out of an adolescent state, this book, or the last part anyway, was a sort of adolescent brainwave. But that didn't matter. What mattered was that when anyone else picked on her book, her mother was up in arms to defend it. All the worry she herself had been going through the last ten days, since the manuscript was foisted on her, vanished as the girl talked. The chief thing was that, in spite of the party-complex and the jazz and the general rebellion against what she thought they called "art," that she was really creative, cared more for what she could reconstruct afterwards of the parties, than of the parties themselves. It shocked her mother, in the book, that the girl should be so concerned with having a drink here and being asked out for a drink there. The idiom upset her, but now here the child was, a very-summer goddess.

"Come again, anytime, day or night. It's quite easy to understand—all these things. Don't be upset about poor Jack. Forget about it, don't even mention it when you see him in the morning." The child waited shy like a little girl. She wants me to kiss her, of course I always want to. But I don't always, because I think maybe she doesn't want it. Those two flower shoulders were under her mother's long hands, the thick hair bound with the blue ribbon close to her face. "There—now run along. But you might like to stay here to-night?" No, she wouldn't spend the night. She would go back to her own little flat. "Hadn't you better ring me up to say you are all right, you have no torch, take mine." No, she would never take the torch after black-out time, she would be all right. "Thank you," she said as if to a kind stranger as the lift-door slid shut.

It would be difficult to sleep now.

– – – – –

Terribly, terribly cold. Actually, the window was open, of course, the covers had slipped off, but in that other dimension there is such a bleak cold. Cold. There they lie, how cold they must be, the flat-stones of the church-yard lie with no distinction like the grave-stones of the Quakers, the Friends. Cold. A wall of the house is down. The wall of our psychic house is down, to let in unknown, uncharted sensation. Everywhere, all the time, in ordinary day-thought is the paralysing fear, but as well there is the vicarious suffering, for those homeless thousands on the Continent.

Even in her dream, she thinks, "it's not only the dead who are cold, it's the living, thousands and thousands in France, Belgium, Holland."

In her dream, standing on the familiar gravel-path of the old church-yard, she thinks "we don't ever realise it, they are so cold." And the stones lie flat, in that homely park-like enclosure where along the sandy paths, she had loi-tered on her way to school (at 6, at 7) and where she had gathered buttercups among the mounds, and stars-of-Bethlehem in the tufts of longer grass by the wooden fence where there were no stones, just humps of grassy earth, where blue soldiers and grey lay alike un-named. Some of them were nursed back to life at the old seminary on Church Street. They had turned the dormitories into hospital wards for the ill and wounded, on the trail back from Gettys-burg on the way to Philadelphia. Those that could not go on, were left behind there, most of them were already nearly gone, but they had cared for blue and grey alike and there they lay with no distinction, with no names. Lost.

Lost? Individually, how lost we are. But I am not lost. Why mama! How cold it is. But is it so cold? She is there, she is in black and I realize that in some vague half-house, open to the air, I am slipping on a black frock. Then over it a dark coat. Around my head, nun-like, I wrap violet and white bands, lest there be no mistake that I am mourning for someone! It must be papa, of course, or papalie, her father, who died when I was 7.

She is there and I kneel before an open fire-place and break twigs and small sticks to place under a dark log. How high now the flame reaches, "this is extravagant," I say, as if we were poor people, peasants, or refugees, mama and I in our rather elegant and not unbecoming mourning. Someone must be propitiated, a housekeeper or our old nurse. Frieda, her name was, she was German. The Germans will be cross? There is this danger? Frieda must not know how much firewood we are using. But we are elegant refugees, I with my bands of white and purple round my forehead. Do we belong in dream, out of time, mama and I, to some religious order? Mother Superior? Mother.

But we are out in the grave-yard again and now it does not seem so cold. Over a wall, climbing over a low roof on the other side, is a branch of white flower. There is a heady, foam-like branch of another white blossom, fruit-blossom, probably. A group of children pass us, look at the wall as if about to break off the flowering branch, "no, no" we say, "you must not touch that branch." No one must touch it, there is summer in mother and daughter, Demeter and Persephone meet here at last.

Married to the dead, she was, wasn't she? Persephone the spring, now married to Death. Here in this graveyard, the dead lie, everywhere the dead are lying and the living fall almost before our very eyes, minute by minute into the channel. Germans? Yes, the terror is never far absent, waking or sleeping, but here in this cold graveyard (in the town of her own and of her mother's birth) lie the rows of flat stones, no titles are indicated on the flat small stones of the early followers of Count Zinzendorf, many of whom left lands and estates in Bavaria, in Saxony, in Bohemia. Small strange names like Job or Zeb are baptized Indians; Indians lie here, at peace too, among the middle-European refugees, the cobbler and the Count.

I am safe now. We built a great fire, brought back a dead log to life, we got warm, she and I together brought back the spring. This war is over, I tell you.

What Do I Love?

MAY 1943

I

You may say this is no poem
but I
will remember this hour
till I die:

the clock from the old bell-tower
says two
but the sun climbing the sky-clock
points noon,

exactly noon; May 14
says the calendar,
and the steps of William's orangery
at Kensington,
become the Venetian doge's water-stair:

exact perfection,
I am 56,
the may-trees blossom:

the wall-door under the chestnut-tree
that I nor anyone else ever saw open,
opens and lets out a carpenter:

he has his chisel,
I have my pencil:

he mends the broken window-frame of the orangery,
I mend a break in time.

II

Do you remember over there,
how a sparrow got caught
in the lily-roots
(fleur-de-lis or water-lily)
of King William IVth's water-trough,
in Dutch William's Dutch garden?

do you remember how you leapt
the fast-locked iron-gate,
and where no profane foot was ever set
(and only the head-gardener's
sacrosanct under-gardener's
favourites might potter)
you untangled the sparrow's foot
from the threads of the lily-root?

III

A canoe slips from under a rhododendron-bush,
or is it Danieli's gondola,
trailing its purple stuff?

the old clock ticks,
but I hear drop-drop of an older water-clock;
the leaves whisper,
or is it a card-game in the orangery?
bright ghosts?
is it sun-light or jets of the candle-points
on the unbroken window-panes?
here is one whole,
here is one nicely set with matchbox wood,
or varnished cardboard,
so the uneven squares make patch-work;
humanity returns
to this exquisite untidy place,

and oddly with humanity the fashionable ghosts
come back;

is it clock-tick?
is it the snip-snap of a snuff-box?
or a patch-box?
is it an older water-clock?
is it the delicate, only-just perceptible whisper
of the hour-glass?

is it a later fashionable hour-glass lady?
or merely a box-tree?
is it a lady in a hoop or is it a box-tree peacock?

this placard announces:
The damage to this room is part of the
destruction caused by German incendiary bombs
dropped on Kensington Palace, 14 October, 1940;

but enemy action has not driven away
the happy ghosts
somehow it has brought them back;

this is not a poem
only a day to remember,
I say the war is over . . .
the war is over . . .

IV

He said (last winter),
these people have the advantage over us,
and I was sorry, God knows I was sorry enough;
the burnt-red of Texas or the sun-burnt bronze
of his Arizona desert
had not had time to wear off,
and the rest of them stood in the rain,
a neat line waiting,

not saying anything,
but he barked from a young angry throat,
these people have the advantage:

so we did, so we had,
we shuffled along in the rain,
a dingy crowd
with fish-baskets, old rain-coats,
funny umbrellas, a motley host,
dim, undistinguished, water-rats
in the water,
land-rats in the gutter.

V

These people have the advantage over us,
did he speak for himself or for
the rest of the bronze giants?
I wanted to stop, slithered along,
web-footed, trying to work out in that moment,
whether it were better to stop, to speak,
but I was embarrassed by the neat row of them,
drawn up on the pavement,
and what would I say anyway?
I wanted to say I was sorry,
actually thinking of them,
not of us.

VI

I wanted to say I was sorry,
but why should I? but anyway
I did want to say I was sorry,
but how could I? who was I?
I wanted to say, yes, we're used to it,
we have the advantage,
you're new to it;
we've slithered so long in the rain,

prowled like cats in the dark,
like owls in the black-out,
look at us—anæmic, good-natured,
for a rat in the gutter's a rat in the gutter,
consider our fellowship,
look at each one of us,
we've grown alike, slithering,
slipping along with fish-baskets,
grey faces, fish-faces, frog gait,
we slop, we hop,
we're off to the bread-queue,
the meat-shop, the grocery,
an egg?—really madam—maybe to-morrow—
one here—one there—another one over there
is heroic (who'd know it?)
heroic? no bronze face—

no

   no

      no
what am I saying?

VII

It was Goldie, that was her vulgar name,
(one of these was her mother);
better move over,
the fire-man said, miss,
getting a bit hot, miss,
(look out

     look out

        wall!)
better run your little bus
around the other side,
cigarette miss?
he offered her a cigarette
because . . . he thought . . . for a minute . . .

he might push her out of it . . .
it's no use Frank, that's Goldie—
what of it? she's a kid,
she's too young—shut up,
all the kids are in it.

Goldie wouldn't move away,
she was told to stay.

VIII

Goldie had her picture
in a little exhibition,
Goldie was in the news
for half a second,
Goldie had her little job,
ambulance?
                    mobile canteen?
                                        extra fire-girl?
I don't know,
I only just remember
the caption,
a line and a half,
below the newspaper photograph,
which said:

known as Goldie
because of her
fair
hair,
she was found sitting upright
at the wheel of her emergency car,
dead.

IX

Goldie was one of us,
we are one with Goldie;

Arizona desert,
Texas and Arkinsaw,
how could you know,
you did not see
what we saw:

Goldie was only one,
Goldie's all around us,
gutter-rats,
land-rats,
look at us,
slop flop,
stop hop,
past Arkinsaw, Kansas
drawn up on the pavement:

no one will tell you;
only I, one of you,
one of them,
know the rune,
only I can play the tune,
make the song,
tell the story
of Goldie:

Goldie made the words come true,
the sun never sets on . . .
anæmic faces in the line
waiting in the bread queue.

X

The reason is:

rats leave the sinking ship
but we . . .
    we . . .

didn't leave,
so the ship
didn't sink,
and that's madness,
Lear's song,
that's Touchstone's forest-jest,
that's Swan of Avon logic:

the ship didn't sink
because
the rats knew
the timber true:

the ship-rats hop flop
along the pavement-deck a-wash,
O Kansas, O Arkansaw

Goldie wouldn't move away,
Goldie was told to stay.

XI

Frog faces,
frog lust,
frog bellies
in the dust,
till unexpected flame
gave you another name:

(there's the siren wail again,
May 15;
by the clock,
near 6,
that's 4
by the sun):

frog faces,
frog lust,
frog bellies
in the dust
of the Last Judgment Day:

when winter-fog is gone,
the frogs sit in the sun,
and now you can see
strawberry-leaves
on a crown,
a lion,
a unicorn:

now you can clearly see
what frogs in the sun
become:

salamanders in the flame,
heraldic wings surround the name
English from Englisc from
Engle, Angle
from the Angles who settled
in Briton.

XII

Now you can clearly see
why I sing this mystery
of Goldie, Angel in the sun,
of Goldie up with the fire-alarm,

now this stocking,
now the other shoe on,
of Goldie who ran and chaffed
the telephone-girl because she laughed

at Goldie lazy
but up with the gong:

sea-nymphs hourly ring his knell
(hers, rather—Goldie's—)
   ding
        dong
              bell.

XIII

Goldilocks, Goldilocks let down your hair,
for we have never seen anywhere
a thread so delicate, spun so fair:

Goldie in a tissue-paper frock
hunts for strawberries in the snow,
or was that another? anyhow

Goldie or Gretel in woolen socks
scatters bread-crumbs to show the way
through the dark forest, or did you say

a Saint with Halo beside a wheel
is set on an altar where people kneel,
to take their bread from a priest, instead

of Gretel who changed her crumbs
for pebbles? the pebbles lay like little shells
under green-boughs that swayed like water,

while over and through it swam sea-girls;
the youngest princess begged feet for fins,
Goldie, Gretel or Saint Catherine?

End

R.A.F.

I

He said, I'm just out of hospital,
but I'm still flying.

I answered, *of course,*
angry, prescient, knowing

what fire lay behind his wide stare,
what fury of desire

impelled him,
pretending not to notice

his stammer
and that now, in his agony to express himself

his speech failed
altogether,

and his eyes seemed to gather
in their white-heat,

all the fires of the wind,
fire of sleet,

snow like white-fire pellets,
congealed radium, planets

like snow-flakes:
and I thought,

the sun
is only a round platform

for his feet
to rest upon.

So I knew his name,
the coming-one

from a far star,
I knew he would come again,

though I did not know
he would come so soon;

he stood by my desk
in my room

where I write this;
he did not wear

his blue tunic with the wings,
nor his cap with the crown;

his flying-helmet,
and his cumbersome trappings

were unfamiliar,
like a deep-sea diver.

III

I had said,
I want to thank you,

he had said,
for what?

I had said,
it is very difficult

to say what I want,
I mean—I want

personally to thank you
for what you have done;

he had said,
I did nothing,

it was the others;
I went on,

for a moment infected with his stammer
but persistent,

I will think of you
when they come over,

I mean—I understand—I know—
I was there the whole time

in the Battle
of Britain.

IV

He came again,
he did not speak;

I thought; he stands by my desk
in the dark,

he is emissary,
maybe he will speak later,

(does he still stammer?)
I remembered

how I had thought
this field, that meadow

is branded for eternity
(whatever becomes of our earth)

with the mark
of the new cross,

the flying shadow
of high wings,

moving
over the grass.

V

Fortunately, there was no time
for lesser intimacy

than this—
instantaneous flash,

recognition, premonition, vision;
fortunately, there was no time,

for the two-edged drawn-swords
of our two separate twin-beings

to dull; no danger of rust;
the Archangel's own fine blade

so neatly divided us,
in the beginning.

VI

He was huddled
in the opposite corner,

bare-headed, curiously slumped forward
as if he were about to fall over;

the compartment was crowded,
I was facing forward;

I said, put your feet up here
and I wedged myself tighter

and dozed off in the roar
and the train rumble.

VII

In the train jolt
our knees brushed

and he murmured, sorry:
he was there;

I knew in the half-daze,
in the drug and drift,

the hypnotic sway
of the train, that we were very near;

we could not have been nearer,
and my mind winged away;

our minds are winged,
though our feet are clay.

VIII

True, I had travelled the world over,
but I had found no beauty, no wonder

to equal the cliff-edge,
the line of a river

we had just passed,
no picture nor colour in glass

to equal the fervour
of sea-blue, emerald, violet,

the stone-walls, prehistoric circles
and dolmens

that I had just left
in Cornwall.

IX

True, we are cold, shivering,
and we ponder on many things,

waiting for the war to be over;
and I wonder,

has he come for me?
is this my particular winged messenger?

or was it tact,
a code of behaviour,

was it only a sort of politeness,
did he "drop in," as it were,

to explain
why he had not come sooner?

X

My thoughts in the train,
rushed forward, backward,

I was in the lush tall grass
by the burning beeches,

I followed the avenue, out of Tregonning,
across the fields to the other house,

Trenoweth,
where friends were staying;

there was the camellia-bush,
the stone-basin with the tiny lilies

and the pink snails; I remembered
the Scilly Islands off the coast,

and other islands,
the isles of Greece

whose stone thresholds (nor Karnak)
were older

than the sun-circles I had just left;
I thought of Stonehenge,

I thought,
we will be saved yet.

XI

He could not know my thoughts,
but between us

the shuttle sped,
passed back,

the invisible web,
bound us;

whatever we thought or said,
we were people who had crossed over,

we had already crashed,
we were already dead.

XII

If I dare recall
his last swift grave smile,

I award myself
some inch of ribbon

for valour,
such as he wore,

for I am stricken
as never before,

by the thought
of ineptitude, sloth, evil

that prosper,
while such as he fall.

London,
17th September, 1941.

CHRISTMAS 1944

I

The stratosphere was once where angels were;
if we are dizzy and a little mad,
forgive us, we have had
experience of a world beyond our sphere,
there—where no angels are;

the angel host and choir
is driven further, higher,
or (so it seems to me) descended to our level,
to share our destiny;

we do not see the fire,
we do not even hear
the whirr and distant roar,
we have gone hence before

the sound manifests;
are we here? or there?
we do not know,
waiting from hour to hour,

hoping for what? dispersal
of our poor bodies' frame?
what do we hope for?
name remembered? faults forgot?

or do we hope to rise upward?
no—no—not to those skies;
rather we question here,
what do I love?

what have I left un-loved?
what image would I choose
had I one thing, as gift,
redeemed from dust and ash?

I ask, what would I take?
which doll clutch to my breast?
should some small tender ghost,
descended from the host

of cherubim and choirs, speak:
'look, they are all here,
all, all your loveliest treasures,
look and then choose—but *one*—

we have our journey now,
poor child—come.'

II

A Dresden girl and boy
held up the painted dial,
but I had quite forgot
I had that little clock;

I'll take the clock—but how?
why, it was broken, lost,
dismantled long ago;

but there's another treasure,
that slice of amber-rock,
a traveler once brought
me from the Baltic coast,

and with it (these are small)
the little painted swallow—
where are they? one, I left,
I know at a friend's house;

and there's that little cat
that lapped milk from my tray
at breakfast-time—but where?

at some hotel perhaps?
or staying with a friend?
or was it in a dream?

a small cat with grey fur;
perhaps you may remember?

it's true I lent or gave away the amber,
the swallow's somewhere else in someone's house,
the clock was long ago, dismantled, lost,
the cat was dream or memory or both;
but I'll take these—is it too much?

III

We are a little dizzy
and quite mad,
but we have had
strange visitations
from the stratosphere,
of angels drawn to earth
and nearer angels;

we think and feel and speak
like children lost,
for one Child too, was cast
at Christmas, from a house
of stone with wood for beam
and lintel and door-shaft;

go—go—there is no room
for you, in this our Inn:

to Him, the painted swallow,
to Him, the lump of amber,
to Him, the boy and girl
with roses and love-knots,
to Him, the little cat
to play beneath the manger:

> *if we are dizzy*
> *and a little mad,*
> *forgive us, we have had*
> *strange visitations*
> *from the stratosphere.*

Bibliography

Baccolini, Raffaella. "Teaching H.D.'s Work in a War Literature Course." In *Approaches to Teaching H.D.'s Poetry and Prose,* 120–26. Edited by Annette Debo and Lara Vetter. New York: Modern Language Association, 2011.

Beach, Sylvia. "Inturned." Edited by Keri Walsh. *PMLA* 124.3 (May 2009): 939–46.

Boehnen, Scott. "'H.D., War Poet' and the 'Language Fantasy' of *Trilogy.*" *Sagetrieb* 14.1–2 (Spring/Fall 1995): 179–200.

Bryher. *Beowulf, a Novel.* New York: Pantheon, 1956.

———. Bryher Papers. General Collection, Beinecke Rare Book and Manuscript Library, Yale University. New Haven, Connecticut.

———. *The Days of Mars: A Memoir, 1940–1946.* London: Calder and Boyars, 1972.

———. *The Heart to Artemis: A Writer's Memoirs.* London: Collins, 1963.

Burdekin, Katharine. *Swastika Night.* 1937. New York: Feminist Press, 1985.

Camboni, Marina. "Not Pity but Love. H.D.'s World War II." In *Red Badge of Courage: Wars and Conflicts in American Culture,* 580–89. Edited by Biancamaria Pisapia, Ugo Rubeo, and Anna Scacchi. Rome: Bulzoni, 1998.

CARE. "History of CARE." February 25, 2013. <http://www.care.org/about/history.asp>.

Christmas Under Fire. Directed by Harry Watt. Crown Film Unit, Ministry of Information, United Kingdom, 1941.

Churchill, Winston. "We Shall Fight on the Beaches." Churchill Centre and Museum at the Churchill War Rooms, London. February 25, 2013. <http://www.winstonchurchill.org/>.

Debo, Annette. *The American H.D.* Iowa City: University of Iowa Press, 2012.

Detloff, Madelyn. "Burnt Offerings or Incendiary Devices? Ambivalence, Trauma, and Cultural Work in *The Gift* and *Trilogy.*" In *Approaches to Teaching H.D.'s Poetry and Prose,* 127–34. Edited by Annette Debo and Lara Vetter. New York: Modern Language Association, 2011.

———. *The Persistence of Modernism: Loss and Mourning in the Twentieth Century.* Cambridge: Cambridge University Press, 2009.

Dobson, Silvia. "Mirror for a Star. Star for a Mirror." Unpublished manuscript. Silvia H. Dobson Papers. Beinecke Rare Book and Manuscript Library, Yale University. New Haven, Connecticut.

———. "'Shock Knit within Terror': Living through World War II." *Iowa Review* 16.3 (Fall 1986): 232–45.

————. "Why Bulldoze Xanadu?" Unpublished manuscript. Silvia H. Dobson Papers. Beinecke Rare Book and Manuscript Library, Yale University. New Haven, Connecticut.

Duncan, Robert. *The H.D. Book*. Edited by Michael Boughn and Victor Coleman. Berkeley: University of California Press, 2011.

DuPlessis, Rachel Blau. *H.D.: The Career of That Struggle*. Bloomington: Indiana University Press, 1986.

Edmunds, Susan. *Out of Line: History, Psychoanalysis, and Montage in H.D.'s Long Poems*. Stanford: Stanford University Press, 1994.

Escape. Directed by Mervyn LeRoy. Performed by Norma Shearer, Robert Taylor, Conrad Veidt, and Alla Nazimova. Metro-Goldwyn-Mayer Studios, 1940.

Farson, Negley. *Bomber's Moon: London in the Blitzkrieg*. New York: Harcourt, Brace, 1941.

Friedman, Susan Stanford, ed. *Analyzing Freud: Letters of H.D., Bryher, and Their Circle*. New York: New Directions, 2002.

————. *Penelope's Web: Gender, Modernity, and H.D.'s Fiction*. Cambridge: Cambridge University Press, 1990.

————. *Psyche Reborn: The Emergence of H.D.* Bloomington: Indiana University Press, 1981.

————. "Teaching *Trilogy*: H.D.'s War and Peace." In *Approaches to Teaching H.D.'s Poetry and Prose*, 135–41. Edited by Annette Debo and Lara Vetter. New York: Modern Language Association, 2011.

Fuchs, Miriam. *The Text Is Myself: Women's Life Writing and Catastrophe*. Madison: University of Wisconsin Press, 2004.

Goodspeed-Chadwick, Julie. *Modernist Women Writers and War: Trauma and the Female Body in Djuna Barnes, H.D., and Gertrude Stein*. Baton Rouge: Louisiana State University Press, 2011.

Graham, Sarah H. S. "'We Have a Secret. We Are Alive': H.D.'s *Trilogy* as a Response to War." *Texas Studies in Literature and Language* 44.2 (Summer 2002): 161–210.

Guest, Barbara. Barbara Guest Papers. Yale Collection of American Literature. Beinecke Rare Book and Manuscript Library, Yale University. New Haven, Connecticut.

————. *Herself Defined: The Poet H.D. and Her World*. London: Collins, 1985.

Halsey, Margaret. *With Malice toward Some*. New York: Simon and Schuster, 1938.

Harrison, Victoria. "When a Gift Is Poison: H.D., the Moravian, the Jew, and World War II." *Sagetrieb* 15.1–2 (Spring/Fall 1996): 69–93.

H.D. *Bid Me to Live*. Edited by Caroline Zilboorg. Gainesville: University Press of Florida, 2011.

————. *By Avon River*. Edited by Lara Vetter. Gainesville: University Press of Florida, 2014.

————. *Collected Poems, 1912–1944*. Edited by Louis L. Martz. New York: New Directions, 1983.

————. *The Gift: The Complete Text*. Edited by Jane Augustine. Gainesville: University Press of Florida, 1998.

————. "H.D. by Delia Alton." *Iowa Review* 16.3 (1986): 174–221.

———. H.D. Letters to Mary Herr. H.D. and Bryher Papers. Bryn Mawr College Library. Bryn Mawr, Pennsylvania.

———. H.D. Letters to May Sarton. Henry W. and Albert A. Berg Collection of English and American Literature. New York Public Library. Astor, Lenox, and Tilden Foundations. New York, New York.

———. H.D. Papers. Yale Collection of American Literature. Beinecke Rare Book and Manuscript Library, Yale University. New Haven, Connecticut.

———. *Helen in Egypt*. New York: New Directions, 1961.

———. "Last Winter." *Poetry* 77 (December 1950): 125–34.

———. "A Letter from England." *Bryn Mawr Alumnae Bulletin* 21.7 (July 1941): 22–23.

———. *Magic Mirror, Compassionate Friendship, Thorn Thicket: A Tribute to Erich Heydt*. Edited by Nephie J. Christodoulides. Victoria, B.C.: ELS Editions, 2012.

———. *Majic Ring (Writing as Delia Alton)*. Edited by Demetres P. Tryphonopoulos. Gainesville: University Press of Florida, 2009.

———. *The Sword Went Out to Sea (Synthesis of a Dream), by Delia Alton*. Edited by Cynthia Hogue and Julie Vandivere. Gainesville: University Press of Florida, 2007.

———. *Tribute to Freud*. New York: New Directions, 1974.

———. *Trilogy*. New York: New Directions, 1973.

———. *Within the Walls*. Iowa City: Windhover Press, 1993.

Henke, Suzette A. "Modernism and Trauma." In *Cambridge Companion to Modernist Women Writers*, 160–71. Edited by Maren Tova Linett. Cambridge: Cambridge University Press, 2010.

Henrey, Robert, Mrs. [Madeline Henrey]. *The Incredible City*. London: J. M. Dent and Sons, 1944.

Herring, Robert. "Editorial." *Life and Letters Today* 32 (January–March 1942): 1–3.

———. "Editorial." *Life and Letters Today* 33 (April–June 1942): 136–42.

———. "Editorial." *Life and Letters Today* 34 (July–September 1942): 153–55.

———. "Editorial." *Life and Letters Today* 37 (April–June 1943): 53–55.

———. "Editorial." *Life and Letters Today* 43 (October–December 1944): 121–24.

———. "Editorial." *Life and Letters Today* 44 (January–March 1945): 121–24.

———. "Editorial." *Life and Letters Today* 48 (January–March 1946): 153-55.

———. "Journal de Guerre." *Life and Letters Today* 26 (July–September 1940): 1–11.

———. "News Reel." 26 *Life and Letters Today* (July–September 1940): 201–14.

———. "News Reel." 28 *Life and Letters Today* (January–March 1941): 104–12.

Hollenberg, Donna Krolik, ed. *Between History and Poetry: The Letters of H.D. and Norman Holmes Pearson*. Iowa City: University of Iowa Press, 1997.

J'Accuse! London: World Alliance for Combating Anti-Semitism, 1933.

Jordan, Viola Baxter. Viola Baxter Jordan Papers. Yale Collection of American Literature. Beinecke Rare Book and Manuscript Library, Yale University. New Haven, Connecticut.

Kluckhohn, Frank L. "African War Over." *New York Times*, May 13, 1943: 1, 3.

Kramer, Ann. *Land Girls and Their Impact*. Barnsley, UK: Pen and Sword Books, 2008.

London Can Take It! Directed by Humphrey Jennings and Harry Watt. GPO Film Unit, Ministry of Information, United Kingdom, 1940.

Mackenzie, Compton. *The Red Tapeworm*. London: Chatto and Windus, 1941.

Moore, Marianne. Moore Papers. Rosenbach Museum and Library. Philadelphia, Pennsylvania.

———. *Selected Letters*. Edited by Bonnie Costello, Celeste Goodridge, and Christanne Miller. New York: Penguin, 1997.

Morris, Adalaide. "Signaling: Feminism, Politics, and Mysticism in H.D.'s War *Trilogy*." *Sagetrieb* 9.3 (Winter 1990): 121–33.

Mrs. Miniver. Directed by William Wyler. Performed by Greer Garson, Walter Pidgeon, and Teresa Wright. Metro-Goldwyn-Mayer Studios, 1942.

Pearson, Norman Holmes. Norman Holmes Pearson Papers. Yale Collection of American Literature. Beinecke Rare Book and Manuscript Library, Yale University. New Haven, Connecticut.

Plank, George. George Plank Papers. Yale Collection of American Literature. Beinecke Rare Book and Manuscript Library, Yale University. New Haven, Connecticut.

"The Poets Speak." *Times Literary Supplement*. April 17, 1943: 187.

Pollard, Robert S. W. *You and the Call-Up: A Guide for Men and Women*. London: Blandford Press, 1942.

Schaffner, Perdita. "A Day at the St. Regis with Dame Edith." *American Scholar* 60.1 (Winter 1991): 113–17.

———. "Canteen Backstage: 2.—W.V.S." *Life and Letters Today* 29 (April–June 1941): 13–23.

———. "Unless a Bomb Falls . . ." In *The Gift* by H.D., ix–xv. New York: New Directions, 1982.

Schaffer papers. Schaffner Family Library. East Hampton, New York.

Schweik, Susan. *A Gulf So Deeply Cut: American Women Poets and the Second World War*. Madison: University of Wisconsin Press, 1991.

Sutton, Walter. "*Trilogy* and *The Pisan Cantos*: The Shock of War." *Sagetrieb* 6.1 (Spring 1987): 41–52.

Willis, Elizabeth. "A Public History of the Dividing Line: H.D., the Bomb, and the Roots of the Postmodern." *Arizona Quarterly* 63.1 (Spring 2007): 81–108.

Index

Bryher: *Beowulf*, 31; on bombing raids, 6, 20, 79, 87, 91; and chickens, raising, 73–74; civilian experience of, 16; clippings on government failures, 74–75; and clothing, wartime, 75–76, 93; on conscription of women, 53; Cornwall visits, 50, 55; *The Days of Mars*, H.D. in, 3, 4; and Dobson, relationship with, 100n154; on Hendersons' flat, bombing of, 91; on food, 66, 71–72, 77–78; friendship with Sitwells, 40–41; and H.D.'s illness, 66–71; and H.D.'s writing, 79; *The Heart to Artemis*, 97n42; on invasion of Europe, 88; at Kenwin, 9–10; *Life and Letters Today*, and, 10; at Lowndes Square, 21; on malnutrition, 74; Nazi atrocities, response to, 9, 38; and Perdita, relationship with, 5, 44, 45; and A Reading by Famous Poets event, 79–82; on scarcity of household items, 76–77; on shopping, 73; Tea Kettle, portrayal of, 31; war activities of, 19–20, 24; and *What Do I Love?*, publication of, 96n7, 96n8; work with refugees of, 9, 21, 38

Bryn Mawr Alumnae Bulletin, 46

Bryn Mawr College, 15, 47, 49, 66, 70

Buckingham Palace, 18, 59

"Bunny" (H.D.), 27, 32–37

Bunny Thunder, 33–34, 35

Burdekin, Katharine. See *Swastika Nights*

By Avon River (H.D.), 4

Camboni, Marina, 95n5

Carcanet, 4

CARE packages, 77–78

Chamberlain, Neville, 10, 17, 32

Children's Overseas Reception Board, 59

"Christmas 1944" (H.D.), 5, 90–92, 95n5, 96n7

Christmas Under Fire, 25

Churchill, Winston, 6, 10, 16, 32; evacuation of Dunkirk, 11; speeches, 12, 15, 19

CIA, 35

City of Benares, SS, 60

Clocks, in H.D.'s work, 28, 30–31, 41, 83, 91; in *What Do I Love?* 155, 156, 157, 162, 174, 175; in *Within the Walls* 111, 126, 143

Cold War, 70, 101n165

Coleridge, Samuel Taylor. See *Rime of the Ancient Mariner, The*

Collected Poems (H.D.), 96n10

Conscription of women, 6, 33, 52–53, 60, 107

Cornwall, 50, 55, 99, 119, 125–26, 170

Cripplegate, 16

Czechoslovakia, 9

Daladier, Édouard, 10

Daylight saving time, 41, 83, 143

D-Day, 6, 88

Debo, Annette, 96n20, 98n89, 101n165

De Gaulle, Charles, 80

De la Mare, Walter, 79

Demeter, 27, 45, 151

Denmark, 10, 17

Detloff, Madelyn, 95n5, 96n5

Dimbleby, Richard, 18

Dobson, Silvia, 5, 9, 23, 27, 42, 49; "bomb alley," location of farm in, 55–56; and evacuating children, 59–60; Lowndes Square description of, 20–21; relationship with H.D., 55–56, 100n154; siblings, 31; and Women's Land Army, 31, 56, 60–62; Woodhall farm, 55, 56, 60, 61, 62

Doodle-bugs, 6, 89, 90

Doré, Gustav, 116

"Dream of a Book" (H.D.), 28

Duncan, Robert, 95n5

Dunkirk, 6, 16; evacuation of, 11–12, 54

Duplessis, Rachel Blau, 96n5

Eckington, Robert Herring's home in, 30, 119, 126

Eddington, Arthur Stanley, 28

Eden, Anthony, 32, 75, 79, 133–34

Edmunds, Susan, 95n5

Egoist, The, 15

Einstein, Albert, 28, 143

Eliot, T. S., 79; *Four Quartets* 42

Stonehenge, 171
Subway tunnels, 22, 23, 25, 29, 30
Summer time. *See* Daylight saving time
Sutton, Walter, 95n5
Swanley Agricultural College, 60
Swastika Nights (Burdekin), 36
Switzerland, 6, 9, 10, 21, 23; Perdita's childhood in, 35, 98n75; post-World War II conditions in, 67, 68, 69, 70; in *Within the Walls*, 129, 145, 148

Tea Kettle, 29, 31, 49
Thames, 13, 30
"Tide-Line" (H.D.), 28
Times Literary Supplement, 79–81
Tolstoy, Leo. See *War and Peace*
Trafalgar Square, 93
Trenoweth, 55, 171
Tribute to Freud (H.D.), 4, 95n5
Tribute to the Angels (H.D.), 4
Trilogy (H.D.), 4, 5, 19, 42, 95–96n5, 96n7; as healing epic, 3
True Woman, 37
Tryphonopoulos, Demetres P., 96n5
Tunisia, 103n233
Turner, W. J., 102n215

United States, 3, 25, 92; support for Britain, 15; in *Autobiography* (Perdita Schaffner), 44; H.D.'s friends in, 5, 6; Moore as H.D.'s literary executor in, 49; rationing in, 82, 84; as refuge, 3, 9, 38, 59; World War II, involvement in, 46, 52
Utility Furniture Scheme, 76

V-1 rocket, 89
V-2 rocket, 89
Vandivere, Julie, 96n5, 101n166
Vaud, 29, 70
V-E Day, 6, 93
Venice, 83, 100n154
Vetter, Lara, 96n5
Vienna, 9, 32, 38, 83, 129, 135

Vittel, 39, 90
Volkart, Elsie, 9, 70

Waley, Arthur, 102n215
Walls Do Not Fall, The (H.D.), 4, 19
War and Peace (Tolstoy), 17
"Warehouse" (H.D.), 30–31, 44
Wellesley, Dorothy, 81–82, 102n215
Wellesley, Lady Gerald. *See* Wellesley, Dorothy Gerald
What Do I Love? (H.D.), 3, 43, 46, 95n5, 103n231; overview, 4–5; publication, 45, 82, 96n7, 96n10
Whitechapel, 18
Williams, William Carlos, 24, 42
Willis, Elizabeth, 95n5
Windhover Press, 4
"Within the Walls" (H.D.), 27
Within the Walls (H.D.), 3, 27, 95n5; overview, 4, 5; time, theme of in, 27–28, 31, 40, 41–42, 107–8, 113–14; writer, theme of in, 27, 28–29, 40, 42–43. *See also* Clocks, in H.D.'s work
With Malice Toward Some (Halsey), 36
Wolle, Francis, 6, 23
Women's Land Army, 6, 31, 56, 58, 59, 60–61
Women's Voluntary Service, 33–34
Women's war work, 6, 32–37
Woodhall, 55–56, 60–62
Woolf, Virginia, 4, 42–43, 141
World War I, 3, 12, 16, 23, 59, 73
World War II, 49, 95–96n5; American involvement in, 46–47, 52; as civilian war, 12, 31; daylight savings time during, 41–42; food during, 71; H.D. as war writer, 3–4; H.D.'s epics on, 42; as "Phoney War," 10; and women's labor, 59
Writing on the Wall (H.D.), 4, 9

Yale University, 4, 44, 96n10

Zilboorg, Caroline, 96n5
Zinzendorf, Count Nicholas Lewis von, 151
Zola, Emile, 38

ANNETTE DEBO is professor of English at Western Carolina University in the mountains of North Carolina. She is author of *The American H.D.* and coeditor of the MLA volume *Approaches to Teaching H.D.'s Poetry and Prose.* Debo is a past cochair of the H.D. International Society and has held the H.D. Fellowship at Yale University's Beinecke Rare Book and Manuscript Library. Her articles have appeared in *African American Review, Callaloo, Paideuma, South Atlantic Review, Quarterly Review of Film and Video, CLA Journal,* and *College Literature.*

CPSIA information can be obtained
at www.ICGtesting.com
Printed in the USA
FSHW01n1016100518
48050FS